ᴇʀ

HIDE

(A May Moore Suspense Thriller —Book Four)

BLAKE PIERCE

D1615983

Blake Pierce

Blake Pierce is the USA Today bestselling author of the RILEY PAGE mystery series, which includes seventeen books. Blake Pierce is also the author of the MACKENZIE WHITE mystery series, comprising fourteen books; of the AVERY BLACK mystery series, comprising six books; of the KERI LOCKE mystery series, comprising five books; of the MAKING OF RILEY PAIGE mystery series, comprising six books; of the KATE WISE mystery series, comprising seven books; of the CHLOE FINE psychological suspense mystery, comprising six books; of the JESSE HUNT psychological suspense thriller series, comprising twenty four books; of the AU PAIR psychological suspense thriller series, comprising three books; of the ZOE PRIME mystery series, comprising six books; of the ADELE SHARP mystery series, comprising sixteen books, of the EUROPEAN VOYAGE cozy mystery series, comprising four books; of the new LAURA FROST FBI suspense thriller, comprising nine books (and counting); of the new ELLA DARK FBI suspense thriller, comprising eleven books (and counting); of the A YEAR IN EUROPE cozy mystery series, comprising nine books, of the AVA GOLD mystery series, comprising six books (and counting); of the RACHEL GIFT mystery series, comprising eight books (and counting); of the VALERIE LAW mystery series, comprising nine books (and counting); of the PAIGE KING mystery series, comprising six books (and counting); of the MAY MOORE mystery series, comprising six books (and counting); and the CORA SHIELDS mystery series, comprising three books (and counting).

An avid reader and lifelong fan of the mystery and thriller genres, Blake loves to hear from you, so please feel free to visit www.blakepierceauthor.com to learn more and stay in touch.

ISBN: 978-1-0943-7721-6

BOOKS BY BLAKE PIERCE

CORA SHIELDS MYSTERY SERIES
UNDONE (Book #1)
UNWANTED (Book #2)
UNHINGED (Book #3)

MAY MOORE SUSPENSE THRILLER
NEVER RUN (Book #1)
NEVER TELL (Book #2)
NEVER LIVE (Book #3)
NEVER HIDE (Book #4)
NEVER FORGIVE (Book #5)
NEVER AGAIN (Book #6)

PAIGE KING MYSTERY SERIES
THE GIRL HE PINED (Book #1)
THE GIRL HE CHOSE (Book #2)
THE GIRL HE TOOK (Book #3)
THE GIRL HE WISHED (Book #4)
THE GIRL HE CROWNED (Book #5)
THE GIRL HE WATCHED (Book #6)

VALERIE LAW MYSTERY SERIES
NO MERCY (Book #1)
NO PITY (Book #2)
NO FEAR (Book #3)
NO SLEEP (Book #4)
NO QUARTER (Book #5)
NO CHANCE (Book #6)
NO REFUGE (Book #7)
NO GRACE (Book #8)
NO ESCAPE (Book #9)

RACHEL GIFT MYSTERY SERIES
HER LAST WISH (Book #1)
HER LAST CHANCE (Book #2)

HER LAST HOPE (Book #3)
HER LAST FEAR (Book #4)
HER LAST CHOICE (Book #5)
HER LAST BREATH (Book #6)
HER LAST MISTAKE (Book #7)
HER LAST DESIRE (Book #8)

AVA GOLD MYSTERY SERIES
CITY OF PREY (Book #1)
CITY OF FEAR (Book #2)
CITY OF BONES (Book #3)
CITY OF GHOSTS (Book #4)
CITY OF DEATH (Book #5)
CITY OF VICE (Book #6)

A YEAR IN EUROPE
A MURDER IN PARIS (Book #1)
DEATH IN FLORENCE (Book #2)
VENGEANCE IN VIENNA (Book #3)
A FATALITY IN SPAIN (Book #4)

ELLA DARK FBI SUSPENSE THRILLER
GIRL, ALONE (Book #1)
GIRL, TAKEN (Book #2)
GIRL, HUNTED (Book #3)
GIRL, SILENCED (Book #4)
GIRL, VANISHED (Book 5)
GIRL ERASED (Book #6)
GIRL, FORSAKEN (Book #7)
GIRL, TRAPPED (Book #8)
GIRL, EXPENDABLE (Book #9)
GIRL, ESCAPED (Book #10)
GIRL, HIS (Book #11)

LAURA FROST FBI SUSPENSE THRILLER
ALREADY GONE (Book #1)
ALREADY SEEN (Book #2)
ALREADY TRAPPED (Book #3)
ALREADY MISSING (Book #4)
ALREADY DEAD (Book #5)
ALREADY TAKEN (Book #6)

ALREADY CHOSEN (Book #7)
ALREADY LOST (Book #8)
ALREADY HIS (Book #9)

EUROPEAN VOYAGE COZY MYSTERY SERIES
MURDER (AND BAKLAVA) (Book #1)
DEATH (AND APPLE STRUDEL) (Book #2)
CRIME (AND LAGER) (Book #3)
MISFORTUNE (AND GOUDA) (Book #4)
CALAMITY (AND A DANISH) (Book #5)
MAYHEM (AND HERRING) (Book #6)

ADELE SHARP MYSTERY SERIES
LEFT TO DIE (Book #1)
LEFT TO RUN (Book #2)
LEFT TO HIDE (Book #3)
LEFT TO KILL (Book #4)
LEFT TO MURDER (Book #5)
LEFT TO ENVY (Book #6)
LEFT TO LAPSE (Book #7)
LEFT TO VANISH (Book #8)
LEFT TO HUNT (Book #9)
LEFT TO FEAR (Book #10)
LEFT TO PREY (Book #11)
LEFT TO LURE (Book #12)
LEFT TO CRAVE (Book #13)
LEFT TO LOATHE (Book #14)
LEFT TO HARM (Book #15)
LEFT TO RUIN (Book #16)

THE AU PAIR SERIES
ALMOST GONE (Book#1)
ALMOST LOST (Book #2)
ALMOST DEAD (Book #3)

ZOE PRIME MYSTERY SERIES
FACE OF DEATH (Book#1)
FACE OF MURDER (Book #2)
FACE OF FEAR (Book #3)
FACE OF MADNESS (Book #4)
FACE OF FURY (Book #5)

FACE OF DARKNESS (Book #6)

IF SHE HID (Book #4)
IF SHE FLED (Book #5)
IF SHE FEARED (Book #6)
IF SHE HEARD (Book #7)

THE MAKING OF RILEY PAIGE SERIES
WATCHING (Book #1)
WAITING (Book #2)
LURING (Book #3)
TAKING (Book #4)
STALKING (Book #5)
KILLING (Book #6)

RILEY PAIGE MYSTERY SERIES
ONCE GONE (Book #1)
ONCE TAKEN (Book #2)
ONCE CRAVED (Book #3)
ONCE LURED (Book #4)
ONCE HUNTED (Book #5)
ONCE PINED (Book #6)
ONCE FORSAKEN (Book #7)
ONCE COLD (Book #8)
ONCE STALKED (Book #9)
ONCE LOST (Book #10)
ONCE BURIED (Book #11)
ONCE BOUND (Book #12)
ONCE TRAPPED (Book #13)
ONCE DORMANT (Book #14)
ONCE SHUNNED (Book #15)
ONCE MISSED (Book #16)
ONCE CHOSEN (Book #17)

MACKENZIE WHITE MYSTERY SERIES
BEFORE HE KILLS (Book #1)
BEFORE HE SEES (Book #2)
BEFORE HE COVETS (Book #3)
BEFORE HE TAKES (Book #4)
BEFORE HE NEEDS (Book #5)
BEFORE HE FEELS (Book #6)
BEFORE HE SINS (Book #7)
BEFORE HE HUNTS (Book #8)

BEFORE HE PREYS (Book #9)
BEFORE HE LONGS (Book #10)
BEFORE HE LAPSES (Book #11)
BEFORE HE ENVIES (Book #12)
BEFORE HE STALKS (Book #13)
BEFORE HE HARMS (Book #14)

AVERY BLACK MYSTERY SERIES
CAUSE TO KILL (Book #1)
CAUSE TO RUN (Book #2)
CAUSE TO HIDE (Book #3)
CAUSE TO FEAR (Book #4)
CAUSE TO SAVE (Book #5)
CAUSE TO DREAD (Book #6)

KERI LOCKE MYSTERY SERIES
A TRACE OF DEATH (Book #1)
A TRACE OF MURDER (Book #2)
A TRACE OF VICE (Book #3)
A TRACE OF CRIME (Book #4)
A TRACE OF HOPE (Book #5)

PROLOGUE

Shawna Harding jogged along the trail leading through the forest, making sure to check behind her before she ran into the woods. Living with a vague, but distinct, level of threat had become normal in the past two weeks. She and her school friends hadn't stopped talking about the girl who'd disappeared a fortnight ago.

They were all feeling scared and unsure, as day after day went by without any news.

Emily Hobbs had always taken the jogging trail that led past the lake. In the past, Shawna had seen her out jogging a few times.

That was why Shawna had changed her route and was now running a different way. Just in case Emily had been grabbed by someone while out on that trail.

As she jogged, enjoying the warmth of the early summer afternoon, she thought about the missing girl. It was possible Emily had run away, but it wasn't likely. Why would she? She was in Shawna's class at Chestnut Hill High, and they had some friends in common. Emily was a popular girl, on three sports teams, and she had been first princess in the local beauty pageant last year. You didn't want to get on her wrong side, though. She wasn't a bully, exactly. She just didn't put up with weakness, which Shawna respected and admired. She also knew that to be successful in life, you had to stand your ground.

Shawna, too, aimed to be a success. She was usually in the top ten in terms of grades. She was captain of the debating team, and on a few sport teams. Her parents were on the school board. Shawna knew her father always said that school prepared you for life, and you had to get used to fighting for what you deserved. There was no point in being a nobody, and sometimes being hard on people was the best way. People needed to be tough in life. That was the take-home message that Shawna had learned from her dad.

But being among a popular group and academically successful brought pressure with it. Shawna couldn't help feeling constantly stressed that she wasn't good enough, wasn't well liked enough.

Deep down, Shawna wondered if Emily felt the same. Was she different from the tough, assured person she seemed to be? Running away sometimes occurred to Shawna, even though she always scornfully pushed the thought aside when she realized how weak it made her seem.

No, Emily was not that person. She would not have copped out. Running away was a cop-out. That was what Shawna's dad said. Someone so successful wouldn't have done such a thing, would they? Not when her path was already set. Everyone knew Emily was going to be a top criminal lawyer one day, like her mother would have been if she hadn't moved to this small town.

Weirdly, Shawna felt as if her life was also already mapped for her, as if it was set out in a route she had to follow, and there could be no major deviations from this route.

It was comforting in a way. But in another way it made her feel trapped. As if she was not in control of her future, and was just following a path others had chosen.

At least out here, jogging, she could choose her own path. Although even that was now restricted, because of Emily. What had happened to her? Shawna wondered. She'd been seen at school, and then she'd vanished. And she did like to run the trails in the afternoons.

At that moment, Shawna heard a voice from behind her.

"Come here, my lovely. Come here."

It was a man's voice, and it was spoken in a weird, cooing tone.

In fact, Shawna's first thought was that this guy was calling his dog back to him. That was what it sounded like. Like calling to a pet.

She glanced around.

But then a shiver went through her as she saw there was no pet in sight. Just a man, standing about twenty yards behind her. He was dressed in running gear. And he was looking directly at her. Calling to her.

In fact, as she turned, he made this clear.

"Yes, honey. I'm speaking to you. Will you come to me just for a moment?"

Shawna didn't reply. She wasn't going to engage with some creepy guy. Tossing her head scornfully, she turned and increased her pace, and then she heard the man shout.

"Wait, my lovely. I just want to talk to you. I'm not going to hurt you."

She glanced back. He was still there, about twenty yards behind her, but he was starting to jog toward her now.

Shawna felt a chill of fear.

Obviously, this guy was not a psycho kidnapper. He didn't look like one. But he didn't look normal, either. She was wary of strangers right now and there was something very creepy about him.

The best thing she could do was run. As far as possible, and as fast as she could, away from him.

She turned, her heart hammering surprisingly fast.

But this guy was also a runner, it seemed. He was keeping pace with her, and she heard him calling again in that weird, wheedling tone. "No need to be afraid, my sweet. I'm just going to talk to you."

What should she do? Shawna felt uncertain, an emotion she wasn't used to. She should stop and threaten him, take his picture on her phone. But the problem was that if she did that, he would catch up with her, and she didn't like the thought of what might happen next. It wouldn't be a good idea. She sensed that very strongly.

Stopping at all didn't seem like a wise decision. It would be better to run, fast. To head for where other people were. Then this creepy guy would have witnesses to his behavior and she could take the photo and make him suffer for having called out to her like she was some disobedient little Jack Russell.

She could hear his footsteps pounding after her, sure and regular on the trail's earthy surface. And she felt another chill, only this time closer to panic.

He was still calling after her.

"Come back here. Don't be afraid."

Shawna accelerated. Now she felt like she was running for her life.

Was this it? Was this man going to catch up with her and harm her, kill her, even?

"Help me!" she called, but with a feeling of doom, she knew nobody would hear her. He'd approached her just as she'd headed down the most deserted section of the trail, the one that led deep into the woods. She hadn't intended to run this far at all. She'd planned to run a couple hundred yards and then turn and retrace her steps. Now she couldn't do that, because he was behind her. He was forcing her further down this trail.

Worse still, she was getting tired. She wasn't used to this speed. Her legs were feeling leaden and her breath was burning in her chest.

And he was still following her, which made her feel sick with fear. In fact, checking again, she saw he was closer now. He was only about ten yards behind her, and then he put on a burst of speed and closed the gap.

He was smiling. She could hear his breathing. In and out, huffing and puffing, but not breathless. Not tired. This was a fit guy who looked like he could run all day.

Terror washed through her.

"Help me!" she called again, but her voice was cracking and she knew nobody would hear her. All she wanted to do was get away.

Now he was closer, even though she was sprinting as fast as she possibly could.

"Shush, shush, it's okay. It's okay. I don't want to hurt you."

He hadn't touched her. But he was trying to crowd her off the path. In terror, Shawna raised her hand, trying to hit out at him. She didn't know what else to do. She'd run into a nightmare. She was deep in the woods, she was alone, and she'd never, ever thought this would happen.

So fast.

She couldn't keep it up. With a gasp that was more of a sob, she dropped back, running slower.

"That's it, that's right. Just take it easy now."

He was pushing against her, holding her wrist in the lightest grasp, as if he was afraid to hurt her in any way, and yet he was implacably herding her the way he wanted her to go.

And she couldn't resist. She couldn't even breathe. She was exhausted from trying to run.

"Please no! Please don't hurt me!" she sobbed out, and with a weird sense of foreboding, she realized she sounded just like the weaklings her father had always warned her not to tolerate. *Don't be a weak whiner, Shawna, don't be one of those who beg and plead. You stand up for what you want and you take it!"*

His advice was useless here, but so was fighting him off. Shawna realized that nothing was going to derail this man from what he intended to do.

"I wouldn't do that. There, there, I'm not going to hurt you. Just come with me. Come this way."

Her legs were shaking. Terror and exhaustion combined had sapped all their strength. Shawna staggered to a stop.

"Did you take Emily? You did, didn't you? You took her. It was you!" She was gasping so hard she could hardly get the words out.

"Don't scream now, my lovely. It's okay."

She didn't scream. She could barely breathe. Her whole body was trembling.

He took her arm, holding her, supporting her.

4

"Look, you're tired. That's okay. Just don't be afraid. Don't be frightened. I'm not going to hurt you. Just hold on to me."

He took her arm, wrapping it around his shoulders. Terrified, she tried to pull away, but his grip, although not rough, was solidly firm and it was impossible to get free. She staggered, feeling her cell phone drop out of her pocket, too tired to reach for it or even think about it.

"Come on. Just a little further."

Shawna felt dizzy with exhaustion and fear. Her legs felt as if they were made of jelly and she kept stumbling. And he was still leading her. She felt trapped. Helpless. She couldn't run and he'd tired her out and now she was his. She'd disappear without a trace, like Emily had.

Shawna feared, with a deep, terrible certainty and despite his breathless, coaxing words, that he was going to kill her.

CHAPTER ONE

Deputy May Moore sat alone in the back office at the Fairshore police department. Working late, she was rereading the missing persons file, frowning down at the information, wishing she could do more to find Emily Hobbs, who had disappeared without a trace two weeks ago.

What had happened to her? Had she run away?

But why would she vanish without a word to her parents? Nothing had been going wrong in her life. She'd been a top student, doing well in sports, and definitely one of the 'in' crowd at school.

The other alternative was that she had been abducted. If so, by whom? It was a difficult possibility to consider seriously in their quiet and safe small-town community, but May knew from personal experience that people could just disappear without a trace. Even in small, and supposedly safe, towns.

May's sister Lauren had disappeared ten years ago. She'd stormed out of the house after a fight with May, and had been seen on the trail going down to Eagle Lake, where some of her possessions had later been discovered. Lauren herself had never been found. She had been eighteen at the time of her disappearance. So was Emily.

May feared that Emily's case might also grow cold.

"Please find her! Find her!" Emily's mother's words resounded in her ears from the tearful phone call earlier today, one of the many that May had fielded over the past fortnight.

"I'll do my best, ma'am," May had promised, just as she'd promised yesterday and last week. She'd found out everything she could, but the truth was, she'd hit a dead end. She was at the end of her resources.

Sighing in frustration that she couldn't do more, she pushed back the strands of blond hair that had escaped from her ponytail, and got up from the desk. It was after seven p.m. and she was the only person left here, apart from the constable manning the front desk.

She was aware of the evening silence, the darkening night, the emptiness of the building that was home to the Fairshore police department, which was always abuzz with activity during office hours.

But working late, and taking on as much as she could manage, was all part of her new responsibility as Tamarack County's deputy. The fact that she was the youngest county deputy, and the first female in this role, made May even more motivated to prove herself.

Having done all she could do about Emily's troubling case, May placed the file back in the locker and took a last look around the back office, making sure everything was neat and tidy and ready for the morning. She felt proud of how well organized the office was, and that they were keeping firm control over their current cases, with every step correctly managed and recorded.

Feeling satisfied that the office was neat and ready for the morning, she switched off the lights and walked out, feeling thoughtful

May knew that part of the reason she put so much into her job was out of a deep desire to prove herself. She knew she would never be able to reach the same heights as her sister, Kerry, who was a super-successful FBI agent. May had flunked out and lost her chance. She'd frozen up in the entrance exam, anxiety crippling her, and had missed the cut by a couple of points.

She'd never forgiven herself for that. She'd had all the knowledge and ability, and had known she was capable and competent enough. But with so many expectations weighing on her shoulders, she hadn't been able to work fast enough through the test at that crucial moment when it counted.

She knew that in her parents' eyes, she would always be second-rate. Kerry was always the highest flyer, the one with the career to be proud of.

As she walked thoughtfully out to her car, May wondered if Kerry was going to be able to help her with Lauren's cold case. May had asked her boss recently if she could reopen the case and Sheriff Jack had agreed. As the county deputy, she wanted to bring her skills and experience to relooking at it, and see if there was anything new to find.

And there was something new. She had found a key in the evidence box that had not been mentioned in the report or listed in the log. May was determined to find out what the key unlocked, or at least try to figure out the wording on the smudged, almost illegible, plastic label. So she'd asked Kerry to work on it with her. She'd sent photos to Kerry to see if she had any ideas, or if there was any software at the FBI that might be able to decipher that blurred, unreadable text.

That had been a month ago. Her sister had said she'd try to help her but that there was a backlog for using the software, and she'd have to wait until it was cleared.

As May walked out of the back office, her phone beeped. She felt excited when she saw her sister had messaged her. Perhaps she'd come up with a solution, and the text could be deciphered. May hoped so, because if the key revealed nothing, she knew she had nowhere else to turn.

"Kerry, please let this be good news," she muttered, as she grabbed the phone eagerly.

Then she let out a disappointed sigh.

The text was about a different topic. It wasn't related to Lauren at all. It was yet another message about Kerry's upcoming wedding.

"Hey, sis, when you get a minute, could you send the number of that guy who does the table decorations? You know, the one who lives up in Pine Hills? Or if you have a chance, perhaps you could get pricing from him and just send that through? Thanks!"

May shook her head.

Nothing on Lauren yet. Just more wedding stuff. Exciting as it was, she had to admit that helping Kerry with her thousands of demands and ideas was pretty exhausting. But she'd promised to help, so she'd do her best.

The whole family was permanently on the run with the preparations for the upcoming nuptials, when Kerry would marry a high-caliber lawyer who was as nice as he was successful.

May had no doubt that Kerry's wedding, which would be held at a venue in the local area, would be the event of the year. The decade, even.

But even though wedding messages were currently interrupting her work at least three times a day, May was determined that she was not going to allow this to derail her focus on her own job.

Unfortunately, so far, all the focus in the world had not helped with finding Emily Hobbs.

As she headed for the locker room where she kept her jacket and purse, her phone rang. It was her boss, Sheriff Jack, on the line.

Quickly, she picked up the call.

"Sheriff Jack?" she said.

"May." His tone was heavy and she knew at once, with a twist of her stomach, that this was bad news even before he spoke the words.

"What is it?" she asked, worried.

"There's been a body found. Down by the lake. Near the old boathouse. You need to get here as soon as you can."

May felt coldness suffuse her. This was complicated. She could hear it in Jack's voice, in that abrupt plea for her to get to the scene as soon as she could.

She feared this meant that it was murder. Jack hadn't said it was Emily Hobbs. Perhaps that still had to be confirmed. Her boss was not one for jumping the gun, and preferred to be cautious when giving out information.

But what had happened? What could have played out? Had Emily's body washed up? Was this going to be confirmed as an accidental death, tragic, but at least giving her family closure?

Scenarios flitted through her mind, but none of them matched that heavy tone she'd heard in Jack's voice that told her this was more than serious.

"I'm going to be there in ten minutes," she promised.

May felt a desperate sense of urgency. She needed to get to the scene as quickly as she could. This was her territory, her area of responsibility, and she knew she needed to be there, to take charge, to get to the bottom of what was happening.

She grabbed her jacket out of the locker, shivering as if a sudden chill had gripped her, even though she knew it was her own nerves that were making her feel cold.

Picking up her purse, she took her car keys from the side pocket and sprinted out, anxiety filling her at what she was going to find.

CHAPTER TWO

May sped down the quiet road that led out of Fairshore and toward Eagle Lake. Dread curdled her stomach, and worries filled her mind about what she might find at the scene.

Someone had died. She knew this without a doubt, from Jack's tone. And she feared that it was murder.

All she could do now was get to the scene to find out more. And while on the way, she could call for further backup.

Quickly, May got onto the phone to Deputy Owen Lovell, her investigation partner.

"Hello, May?" He sounded surprised that she was calling him, and instantly, in his voice, she heard a note of the same worry that had been in hers.

"There's been a body found at the lake. Near the old boathouse," she said.

She heard his gasp.

"I'm on my way," he said, and cut the call.

That was what she liked about Owen. Actually, there was much to like about her tall, good-looking deputy who had made a career move to join the police a couple of years ago, wanting to make a difference. But one of the things May most appreciated about him was his ability to pick up on her thinking and do what needed to be done.

He knew this was not the time for questions, since May was clearly in her car and driving at top speed, but rather time to rush to the scene.

As she drove, she tried to calm her nerves, but she felt jumpy and agitated.

The old boathouse was one of the landmarks around town. It was a historical spot, and tourists regularly visited it to photograph it for its picturesque quality, and to see the nature of the remains of the construction.

Some people even dived off the nearby pier, although others said it was too dangerous to do so.

Never before had it been the scene of a crime.

May had never even had to respond to a call from that area, except for a few cases of people getting drunk on boats and needing to be helped back to shore.

Now, as she approached, she saw flashing lights, bright in the darkening surroundings. Clouds had covered the setting sun, creating a somber and gray evening that seemed appropriate somehow.

May parked next to the police cars, noticing a few other vehicles nearby. She climbed out and headed down the hill.

There was the boathouse. Its weathered boards were lovingly maintained by the town's arts committee, who also cut the grass and kept the area beautiful. It was a peaceful, scenic place, usually.

Now, May's heart was in her mouth as she headed over to the scene.

She saw the police were standing right at the water's edge. So was it a drowning? Or had a body been dumped in the lake? She wasn't sure what to expect, and felt filled with trepidation at what was playing out.

"Back, please. Step away," Sheriff Jack was saying to the small crowd of onlookers who were staring, hypnotized, at the water.

Feeling this was getting stranger and stranger, May hurried toward them.

And then she drew in a shocked breath as she saw what they were looking at.

The body of a young girl was in the water and May saw immediately, with a clench of her heart, that it was Emily Hobbs. She'd committed her pretty features and dark hair to memory over the past weeks.

But the scene was beyond bizarre.

Emily was laid out on a makeshift wooden raft, clothed, staring sightlessly at the sky.

Candles were placed around her body. They were no longer lit, and had clearly burned out or blown out in the breeze, but all the same, May felt absolutely shell-shocked by the sight. She could not stop staring, her anger rising as she wondered who had orchestrated this overdramatic murder scene.

And why?

Already, one of the police officers had waded into the dam, dressed in PPE, and was carefully guiding the raft through the waist-deep water and closer to shore.

May had so many questions. But given the sheer bizarreness of the scene, all she could do was watch in silence as the police officer somberly pushed the raft in to shore with his gloved hands.

"I've never seen anything like this before," Sheriff Jack said quietly to her. "I have no idea what kind of person we could possibly be dealing with."

"Me either," she whispered back.

"I notified Emily's parents immediately. So that job's done." May guessed that had been a gut-wrenching task. She was glad her boss had done it.

"Keep everyone back," he advised.

May turned, noticing to her dismay that the crowd was growing. Word about this haunting, disturbing scene was quickly spreading and she knew it would take a team effort to keep back the crowds.

At that moment, Owen arrived at a run. She turned, glad to see her investigation partner on the scene, and that he could help her with keeping the onlookers under control, and preferably, removing them from the area.

"Please keep back from the scene," May said firmly. "If you are not here in an official capacity, it will be best to leave. We need to make space for our emergency workers."

She looked sternly at the onlookers, who all looked away, embarrassed to have been caught out gawking. Taking in the situation immediately, Owen turned to the crowd along with May.

"Leave the scene if you're not involved," he said, stepping toward them and forcing them to step further back, allowing the other police to get the crime scene tape in place.

"And no photos!" May added hurriedly, seeing an opportunistic twenty-something-year-old with a phone in his hand. "There are family members we need to consider here. There may be legal implications for the investigation. Put your phones away, and give us some space!"

Reluctantly, the people turned and shuffled away. May heard conversations in low voices, whispered words all around her, as the townsfolk headed back to their vehicles, discussing that shocking scene.

Turning back, May saw that Andy Baker, the pathologist for the area, was already at work. Wearing plastic covers over his boots, he knelt down in the muddy shallows to begin his examination of this body. With it getting dark, Sheriff Jack was directing spotlights to be set up. May knew they would need them, because Andy might be here another hour at least.

Finally, May's investigator's brain began moving again.

Timelines were the first thought she had.

Emily had gone missing two weeks ago. But this body was most definitely not two weeks old. May was going to guess that it was not more than a day old, although she knew Andy could tell more clearly.

So she had been held somewhere, and then killed. How, May wasn't sure. There were no obvious signs.

It was the creepiest thing she'd ever seen.

And as spine-chilling as this tableau was, May knew the harsh truth of it was that she would be in charge of the investigation, as the county's deputy. It would be up to her to figure out who had done this, and why.

There was no time to waste. May knew that every moment counted now and that this case would test her skill in ways she hadn't yet imagined.

Someone had created this scene. Who had done so and why?

It was sending a message, but May couldn't see what it was saying, or why.

She needed to urgently hunt for clues—both physical clues at the site itself, and also the more invisible clues that might be picked up through questioning.

For now, the site needed to be examined first. Perhaps the killer had left a trace behind.

CHAPTER THREE

"I can't believe this, May," Owen muttered to her. "This is the weirdest crime scene I've ever seen."

While the pathologist was finishing his work, the two of them were pacing around the boathouse area, carefully searching for any clues or evidence. This raft could have been launched elsewhere, May knew, but it could also have been pushed out into the water nearby. Evidence at the scene might lead back to the killer. They could not afford to miss anything that was there.

"I can't believe it either. This is just mind-boggling. I hope we can find something to link back to whoever did this."

"It's like an elaborate stage for a play," Owen muttered, echoing May's own thoughts.

The two of them were working together, searching the area in ever-widening circles, trying to find anything that could help them.

Overhead, clouds were gathering and the night was growing darker. A wind was starting to blow strongly, and the trees creaked and moaned.

Her mind was racing. What had it taken to plan, to build, to launch such a strangely significant funeral scene? What did it mean, why had the killer done this, and who was he, or she?

"Do we even know how Emily died?" Owen asked, as they paced along the riverbank, scanning the ground for any sign of footprints, for any splinters or scuff marks that could have come from the homemade-looking raft.

"No. I hope Andy finds out more by the time we get back."

"I hope we find something along the way."

The well-trimmed grass looked pristine, though dry, May saw. She switched her flashlight on, and Owen did the same, but as May searched, she started to suspect that there was nothing here to find.

The lake was huge and there were miles of shore frontage that the killer could have chosen in the nearby area. If he had come to the boathouse for a reason, May was sure the tracks would be nearby, but she couldn't even see any small signs.

As she walked with Owen, she did feel relieved that the relationship between them felt ninety percent back to normal.

Ten percent awkward, May could cope with.

It was better than totally, one hundred percent, off the scale awkward, which it had been for a short while after he'd asked her on a date.

May's face still flamed at the thought of it. It had been so unexpected. He'd been so embarrassed. She hadn't realized he was asking, and had then been mortified by how she'd handled the entire debacle.

Now they were back on an easier footing.

May hoped that in time, she could think about the dating idea again and consider it in a calm light, without all those memories flaring up again.

There were pros and cons to it. The pros were that Owen was definitely on the same wavelength as May. They were good friends, they thought the same way. They shared the same values. May admired Owen's integrity and his dedication to the job, and his intelligence. Also, he was definitely cute.

But the cons were more complex. Being in a romance would change things. Ever since her divorce five years ago, after a short marriage that had been a disastrous mistake in every way, May was scared of going down the same destructive path again.

And what if it affected their ability to work together and she lost the harmonious partnership with her trusted co-investigator?

May had to stop herself sighing aloud as she considered how many factors there were to worry about. It was better to forget about them all, and make sure she was one hundred percent immersed in this important investigation.

Having paced carefully over the grass, May and Owen turned their attention to the boathouse itself.

Now, in the darkening evening, with the wind gusting and the clouds obscuring the moon, the little wooden boathouse had an eerie, abandoned feel.

There was a short wooden jetty, and they both walked out to it.

But May could see nothing along its painted boards. She had a feeling there was nothing to find.

"Let's go back and see if Andy has anything to tell us," May said.

Feeling disappointed that the search of the area had yielded nothing, and that the surroundings looked undisturbed, she headed back.

Andy and his team were working under floodlights, too. Emily's body had been removed from the raft and placed on plastic sheeting on the grass. From there, May knew, it would be transferred to a body bag and taken to the pathologist's office. The raft itself was also going to be transported to the police department. Three gloved officers were busy carefully lifting the crude wooden structure, wrapping it in thick sheets of plastic.

May knew that this could hold important evidence. The way the wood had been cut, the nails used—everything might add up and point the way to the killer.

Even the candles were being carefully removed from the wood and individually bagged.

May stepped forward to speak to Andy.

"Do you know how she died?" she asked. "Are there any signs at all?"

He raised his eyebrows from behind his mask.

"It looks as if she was suffocated or smothered somehow. But there are no signs of a struggle so I am wondering if she was sedated, given some kind of medication first. I'm going to check the blood and run the toxicology report to see if I can get a clearer picture."

"There's no sign of a struggle?" May said.

"No. Absolutely no sign. Not as much as a broken nail. No bruising. So whatever was done, it was done in a way the victim didn't fight it. And her body does not look starved or dehydrated. She must have had access to food and water in the weeks since she went missing."

May shook her head. This was all extremely disturbing. An undamaged body, a bloodless death, no evidence of trauma or struggle.

And then, finally, she noticed something unusual. It was just the tiniest blip in the picture of this otherwise perfect, yet macabre, scene.

"Look there, look at her feet, Andy," she said.

He stared in the direction she was pointing.

"She's wearing mismatched shoes. That's strange, isn't it? One shoe looks much smaller."

They were both white sports shoes. But one was bright white and larger. The other was scuffed, a different model, and smaller.

"Yes. That's a good point." Andy moved closer, looking down at the shoes. "They are definitely different, and I would say the one on her left foot is the correctly fitting shoe. The one on the right looks to be much too small."

"What could that mean?" May wondered.

"I don't know. The whole scene looks strangely ritualistic so maybe this is a part of it. I won't remove the shoes here. I'll wait until I've got her inside, so we don't miss any evidence that might be on, or in, them. But I'm glad you saw that as I'll prioritize it," he said.

"Thank you."

It was a tiny clue, but May felt it was important. It was part of this staged scene.

It was a message from the killer who had sent them this puzzle that as yet, she barely understood.

It was time to probe deeper into who could have done this, and that meant speaking to the people who were close to Emily.

"I can't help feeling that there must be something here, something we're missing," she said. "Some piece of evidence that will point us in the right direction on this one," she said, almost to herself.

She cast her mind back over the case file. All the interviews and phone calls had been listed in the records.

But there had been just one interview still outstanding, one family member who had been elusive. May had noted it earlier, and resolved that she was going to follow up on it as soon as she could in case he was avoiding them for a reason.

She turned to Owen.

"I know it's late, but we need to get going with this. Do you want to come with me to do an interview?"

He nodded. "Of course. The sooner we can make a start, the better."

Turning away from the scene, May headed up the hill to her car.

This was the first step to getting answers. And they would hopefully be able to speak to someone close to Emily who had not been available for questioning when she'd disappeared, as he'd been away. But he had also not come forward to be interviewed afterward. The rest of the family had done so eagerly.

May hoped that tonight they could finally pin down Emily's brother Gordon. Perhaps he held clues that could take them further.

CHAPTER FOUR

"I was rereading the case notes tonight, just before I got the call about Emily's body being found," May told Owen as soon as they were in the car. "And I realized that Gordon never came forward to be interviewed."

Owen blinked. "You're right. He never got back to us."

"We interviewed her parents at least three times, her aunt, her schoolteacher, and her younger brother. But we never spoke to Gordon properly. With all the other interviews and information we had, we didn't chase him down. Now I'm wondering."

"You think he was avoiding us?"

"I don't know. It could have just been that it was too painful for him to talk about his missing sister when he had no real information to add. But it could also be that he was protecting her, and himself, from getting into trouble. You know how people sometimes behave when the police start asking questions, if they've been doing something they don't want the police knowing about," May thought out loud. "Now that there's been a murder, it might be very important to find out if he was doing anything."

In fact, May was kicking herself for not pursuing him earlier. What if he'd had vital information?

"I did try and contact him again the day before yesterday," Owen remembered. "He was still away on vacation at the time. On some sort of hunting trip, I think. He said he was getting back today, but now I think about it, he did sound evasive when I spoke to him. He couldn't give me an exact time when he'd be available."

"All the more reason why we need to speak to him now," May resolved.

They knew the route to the Hobbs' home well. They lived in a sprawling house in a gated estate on the edge of Chestnut Hill. The first time May had been there to speak to Gordon, she'd been told he lived in the cottage on the side of the house, with its own entrance, but that he was away.

May turned off the main road and took the winding route that led to Chestnut Hill, one of the larger lakeside towns. As she drove, she could see lights from the town twinkling in the darkness.

"I hope we can speak to him," Owen said.

May turned up the short road where the Hobbs' home was located. She could already see that there were several vehicles parked outside the main house. She recognized the car belonging to the local pastor, and guessed that a few of the friends and neighbors had rallied round at this tragic time.

Yet again, May felt a guilty clench of her stomach. They'd tried their hardest! But a young woman had died.

If only they'd been in time to save her. Now, all she could do was find the killer.

"Look!" Owen pointed, and May felt her pulse quicken.

The driveway leading to the side cottage, which had been empty last time they'd arrived, now had a car parked there.

The taillights were on. Hopefully, that meant either Gordon had just gotten back from somewhere, or was just going out.

At last they could speak to him and learn what he knew.

May accelerated into the driveway and parked behind the white Audi.

A young man, tall and lean with a shock of dark hair, was unloading bags from the back of the car. The taillights caught his expression. May thought he looked harassed and upset.

"Good evening," May said, getting out of the car. "Mr. Gordon Hobbs?"

"Yes. That—that's me, Officers," he said uncertainly, his gaze veering between her and Owen.

"Our condolences on the news about your sister," May said sympathetically, but she was watching him closely.

He shook his head. "I can't believe it. This whole thing has just been such a catastrophe."

"I'm sure you are rushing to get to your family, but I would appreciate a quick word. We have a few facts to confirm."

Now she thought Gordon looked uneasy.

"Look, I don't know what I can say. I don't know why any of this happened. My sister was just—just amazing. She was so strong. I mean, she was a real leader."

"Do you know of anyone who might have wanted to harm her?" Owen asked.

Gordon frowned. "I don't know. Everyone respected her. She was the most wonderful person."

"You didn't give us a statement. If I remember, we asked the whole family to come forward and give a statement after she disappeared," May said.

"I know. I—well, I was busy, I'd been away on two trips."

"And you didn't get back to us because you were away?"

"I—it has been a hectic couple of weeks," Gordon admitted. "I'm sorry, I didn't realize I should have come forward."

May could see from his expression that he was hiding something. She didn't trust his body language at all. Suddenly, he wasn't making eye contact with her.

He turned away and opened the car door and took out a bag, which he let fall on the ground.

"I really have to get inside now—I mean, to be with my family. I don't know anything more. I can't help you," he added.

"I think you might be able to," May suggested. "Perhaps there's something you have forgotten about that could be helpful?"

She wasn't going to accuse him outright, but she also was not going to back down, she decided.

"I don't think so," Gordon said. "I don't know anything. I loved my sister. I don't know who would do such a thing to her."

May sensed she was nearing the truth. He was hiding something. And the way he'd shuffled his feet as he said that last statement made her want to probe that much more closely.

"Please," Gordon said, looking down. "I need to get inside."

"Before you go..." May didn't speak loudly, but all the same, her words stopped his shuffling feet in their tracks. "Are you sure you don't know who would do such a thing to her?"

He stared at her, wide-eyed and looking guilty.

"You do know that if we investigate, and we find out through other sources that you knew something which you didn't tell, that would also make you liable for criminal charges? Plus, of course, on a personal level, there would be the issue you hadn't been honest about something that could have helped us find your sister's killer."

Now Gordon looked appalled. He stared at them wordlessly. The silence stretched out.

"Okay," he capitulated. "There was one thing. A small thing, but it bothered me. The only thing is, if I tell you, will you tell my parents?"

May shook her head. "You're not underage. Unless we have to reveal it as evidence during the investigation, anything you say to us is confidential."

Gordon sighed. "Well, there was this one time, about three weeks ago. Emily and I, we went out, looking for—looking for a bit of weed. You know, I don't smoke often but I was going to this party, and she came along with me for the ride. For the adventure."

"Okay?" May said. Now she felt they were getting somewhere.

"We didn't really know how to do it because, genuine, I'm not that kind of person." He lowered his head and fidgeted, looking miserable.

"Go on," May encouraged.

"We went to the back end of town, near the industrial area by the river, because that's where we heard the dealers hang out. There was this guy, and we approached him and asked about buying. But he wasn't a dealer. He said he couldn't sell to us. Only he didn't walk away, he then started following us."

"Is that so?" May said.

"He was, like, trying to talk to Emily. It was very creepy. I didn't feel good about it. And I didn't tell my parents, because of why we were there." He looked miserable again. "When she disappeared, I sort of wondered if he'd come along and harassed her or grabbed her, or if he'd been involved somehow. I even went looking for him, but I couldn't find him. I have been worrying about it. Because he was creepy and very persistent. But when I couldn't find him I thought to myself that he must have left town, or gone somewhere else, and that I was just being over-anxious about it because she'd disappeared."

"Can you describe this man?" May asked.

Gordon shrugged. "He was youngish, mid-twenties, I guess. Dark blond hair that didn't look clean, and was tied in a ponytail. And he had a faded denim jacket on. He had a bit of a beard on his face. He wasn't that tall. He looked sort of shabby."

He was frowning. May thought he was trying as hard as he could to give an accurate description.

"And you saw him behind the warehouses?"

"Yes. In that area of town."

"You didn't see him anywhere near your home after that?"

"No. I only saw him the once. But as I say, it was creepy. It made me feel bad."

May nodded.

"Thanks. If we need anything else, we'll come by again. Go to your family now."

Looking overwhelmed, Gordon turned and, picking up his bags, half-ran to the side gate.

"What now?" Owen asked May. "We need to find this guy, right? Where do we start?"

"Let's start by finding out if he has been reported to the police at all. He sounds like a drifter. I know a few of them do stay in that area in summertime, and generally people are aware of them, and do call in any reports. You know how people like that are always being reported for trespassing, even when they're not, because the locals don't trust how they look."

"True," Owen said. "I guess the Chestnut Hill police would know more."

"Let's check with them and see if any locals have alerted them. What Gordon was saying about him following Emily is very suspicious," May said.

CHAPTER FIVE

May was convinced that a drifter in a small-town area like Tamarack County would be known to the local police. There were seasonal drifters who frequented the town, taking up odd jobs or helping out locally. In winter, there were very few in their area, but May, and all the local police, knew that in summer, their numbers increased. And correspondingly, so did petty crimes. It was just the way things were, and there was often frustratingly little they as police could do.

The Chestnut Hill police department was just five minutes away. It was halfway between the exclusive residential area and the less attractive and more industrial side of town.

"At least we got a clear description of him," Owen said. "That will be helpful."

"I think he must have made an impression on Gordon," May agreed.

Within her, she couldn't help the nagging fear that if they had managed to pin down Gordon earlier, they might have learned about this man sooner. If they had, could a death have been avoided?

She pulled up outside what was one of Tamarack County's busier police departments, feeling stressed. At this hour, there were still two officers on duty inside. The crackle of radios told May that others were attending to a burglary in the area.

"Good evening, May and Owen," the closest officer, who knew her well, greeted them.

"Good evening, Howard," she replied.

"Terrible about Emily. We have been fielding so many calls. Was it true she was found out on a raft on the lake? Like a ritual sacrifice, people have been saying. They're scared of witchcraft in the area. Devil worship. People have been calling us with all sorts of concerns."

May nodded.

"Yes, that version is true. We're trying to find out the circumstances. There's no evidence of any witchcraft or devil worship so far. But we do have a possible link to a drifter who might have been reported in your area."

"Who's that?" Immediately, Howard turned to his computer. "Being summertime, we've had a few reports."

"This would have been in the warehouse area."

"Most of them are in that general location. Who are we looking for?"

"Mid-twenties. Dark blond ponytail. Some stubble, short beard, faded denim jacket."

Howard frowned at the screen.

"I think I know who he is. He matches the description of a man who was detained a few days ago for trespassing at one of the local businesses." Howard was reading from the computer. "At Van Tassel's Wholesale, in the industrial area. He was let off with a warning. We took a copy of his ID. His name's Joey Robbins."

He glanced up at May.

"So that description matches?" she asked.

"He sounds like the one. Looking back, I see I have a couple of reports of him from a few days previous to that. It was residents calling in. They said that a shifty-looking man was playing the guitar outside Tammy's Diner. We asked for a description and we got a similar picture. They sounded angry that he was playing it really badly. We contacted the diner and we agreed there wasn't much that could be done, as he was doing it on a public street. They said he often came in and spent the money on food."

"If that's the case, he might be there now," May said.

"Yes. The reports have trickled in from five p.m. to about eight p.m."

May turned to Owen.

"Let's head there now," she said. "If we're lucky, we might find him, and if not, we can ask them to call us when he does appear."

She hurried out.

*

Ten minutes later, May and Owen pulled up outside Tammy's Diner. This was a festive eatery, located on the main road in Chestnut Hill. Being on the main road, the restaurant often attracted its share of passing trade and outsiders.

Tammy's had been a success for decades. It was one of the oldest family-run businesses in Chestnut Hill, now in its third generation of ownership under Tammy Junior, the original owner's granddaughter. May remembered how much Lauren had loved eating there. It had been

24

her favorite place. She'd even had her eighteenth birthday dinner there a couple of months before she'd disappeared.

The diner was a big, attractive building, designed like an old-fashioned railroad car, with lots of wood, glass, and chrome.

May saw Tammy's brother, Vernon, a big solid man, standing watchfully at the door as they parked.

It was about two miles from the warehouses, so it was no surprise to May that this drifter had found his way here. She hoped that he would make an appearance, or else that they would know where he was. Vernon was usually pretty good about keeping track of people who represented a threat to the family business.

Tammy Junior herself was behind the counter and May glimpsed her as soon as they climbed out of the car. A large, cheerful woman in her forties, she was a big, friendly presence in the diner, and there were always customers who came for the food and stayed for Tammy's ready welcome.

But what she didn't see was any sign of Joey Robbins.

Returning Tammy's wave from inside before she rushed over to help another customer, May and Owen headed over to speak to Vernon.

"Evening, Deputies," he said solemnly. "How can I help? Are you here to dine, or is this about the case?" He didn't even need to say what case. Clearly, everyone in the diner had been talking about it already.

"It's connected with the case. We believe a man called Joey Robbins has been here recently. He's a drifter who's been playing the guitar to earn dinner money?"

Vernon nodded. "Yes, Joey. I've been keeping a close eye on him. He's trouble, I can see it."

"What's he been doing?"

"He's been coming here at odd hours. Playing the guitar appallingly. He tried to chat up a few of the women heading inside, which I put a stop to immediately. I know the law. I told him if he wants to play, and he stays on the sidewalk, we won't interfere. But if he starts soliciting customers, I warned him that he could expect trouble."

May wouldn't have wanted trouble from six-foot-two Vernon.

"He said he's a handyman, but there's no evidence of that."

"Thank you, Vernon. We're looking for him to question him."

"Is he connected to Emily's death?" Vernon looked concerned.

"We don't have proof of that, but we need to confirm where he was at the time of the crime. Do you know where he stays?"

"Yeah, I do know, because on the night when he tried to chat up one of our customers, I escorted him home," Vernon said firmly, pointing across the road. "He's set up a tent on the vacant plot of land just down there. You know, by the sand road, near the construction site where the new apartments are being built? If he had anything to do with Emily's death, I hope you arrest him and he never sees the outside of a jail cell again," Vernon promised.

"Thank you," May said. "If he's anything more than a harmless drifter, we'll be arresting him immediately."

With another wave to Tammy, she and Owen rushed across the road together.

Now that they knew where Joey was located, there was no time to lose in speaking to him.

May could see the construction site ahead, a dusty place with barriers in place cordoning off the working areas. At this time of night, there were only a couple of trucks still busy, and operations were wrapping up for the day. A few construction workers in reflective vests were walking through the site.

To the right of this site, May saw the area of vacant land where the opportunistic Joey had set up camp. There it was, a pale green tent, surprisingly large.

And there was someone walking to it. Her heart quickened. This must be him. Now they could find out what he'd been up to, and whether there was any evidence on his person or in his tent linking him to this crime.

"Joey Robbins?" May called, getting close enough to see the paleness of the denim jacket in the gloom. "We're police officers. We'd like to talk to you."

The man looked around. In the muted glow of the streetlight, May could see he looked appalled to see them there.

Without hesitating or even speaking a word to them, Joey turned and ran, bolting down the sand alleyway between the vacant land and the construction site.

CHAPTER SIX

May ran after Joey Robbins as fast as she could. There wasn't a moment to waste, because this man was a drifter, a person who had no ties or connections to this town, and could disappear as swiftly as he'd arrived.

If she didn't catch him now, there was a strong chance he would melt away, hiding from the law for weeks or months or even forever. And the fact he was running already proved that he was not an innocent man.

"Stop!" she yelled.

She charged after him. With her boots pounding in the red dust, she sped along the road, pushing herself hard, faster and faster.

"Stop!" she yelled again.

He was fast, she had to give him that. He was sprinting like lightning over the uneven ground, and probably knew this terrain much better than she did, considering he'd been living here for a couple of weeks.

"Joey Robbins, we need to speak to you!" she yelled again, because he was still running.

She forced herself to run with the speed and purpose of her prey, because she knew she could simply not afford for him to outpace her. He had to be stopped, and she had to do it. She couldn't let him get away.

May knew she had to trust in herself and in her own fitness and training. She went for runs on the lakeside trails three times a week. She was fast over uneven ground, and she needed to believe she was fit enough to keep pace with him. Surely he couldn't keep up this speed, not once the adrenaline rush of seeing the police had abated.

She ran hard, trying to stride confidently over the rough terrain, letting her body find the right rhythm and her eyes focus on what could be seen in the near-blackness.

"Mr. Robbins! We need to speak to you!" Owen yelled, pounding behind her. She felt massively grateful for his backup, and that he was there with her. Her deputy was flinging himself headlong into this pursuit with the same determination as she was.

27

Joey veered to the right, heading toward the sandy parking lot and the construction site. May picked up the pace, fixed her attention on his pale denim jacket, moving ahead of her. She realized with a twist of anxiety that she wasn't going to get to him fast enough. He was going to flee into the site. He must have a plan in mind, but she couldn't work out what it was. It was very possible there was a route out the back of the site that he knew about. In the dark, in this big, chaotic area, it would be very easy for him to lose them. The back of the site led into the built-up area of town, with high-density offices, alleyways, and no shortage of hiding places.

With a surge of effort, she picked up her pace and ran down the slippery, sandy incline into the site itself. Her breathing was ragged, but she knew she couldn't stop yet. She had to outrun him. Or outmaneuver him. Or preferably both. At any rate, by the time she left this site, it needed to be with Joey Robbins in her custody.

The site was lonely and semi-dark. Only the chugging of one or two vehicles could be heard in that lonely place. Most of the spotlights were turned off now, with only a couple left shining near the entrance, and in the area that was still being flattened. The drone of machinery grew louder as they approached.

Joey glanced behind him and saw that she was gaining on him. In the glow from a spotlight, she saw his face was anxious and drawn, but he wasn't slowing down. May was filled with self-doubt. She was going to be too slow. She was going to fail.

Panic filled her at the thought he might get away.

And then, to her astonishment, she saw him dart toward the southern section of the construction site, where an old, dusty pickup was parked.

As he got closer and closer to the pickup, May realized in shock that he was going to use it as a getaway vehicle. Most likely, it would be parked with the keys inside, being on site. She knew how things were in this industry.

Driving it even for a few miles would give him the lead he needed to lose them. He could abandon it near a train station, or a busy downtown intersection, jump out, and simply disappear.

She could see his expression as he reached the car. He was terrified and desperate to escape, but there was also a look of maddened determination.

May thought frantically. Speed alone would not save the situation now. He was too far ahead of them. It would be wrong to use her gun at such a time and in any case, it was too dark and he was too far away to take a safe shot.

Instead, intelligence and forward thinking could give her the edge she needed.

"The gate, Owen! Go to the gate!" she yelled.

If the gate was closed in time, he couldn't leave the site. There might be other bolt holes for a running man to use, but there was only one way trucks could get in and out.

She didn't even waste a moment turning to look. She trusted Owen, and knew that he would pick up on her thinking, veer off to the left, and get to the main vehicle gate as fast as he could.

And in the meantime, she was going to see if she could catch Joey Robbins before he got that truck into gear and sped away.

May pushed aside all traces of her own self-doubt. She was fast enough. Smart enough. And she was going to be strong enough to catch this fugitive who was fleeing from them in such a cowardly way.

Putting everything into her efforts, she raced toward him and saw she was gaining on him again. He climbed into the truck's cab, but as he did, in his own panic, his foot slipped.

May reached him and leaped for him, grabbing the back of his jacket with her fist even as he tried to scramble inside.

She yanked him round and hurled herself at him, pushing him up against the truck's body.

"Ow," Joey whimpered. He looked astonished as she shoved him and pinned him against the side.

May was breathing so hard she could barely get any words out. Joey was panting so fast he couldn't say anything coherent at all.

"You're under arrest," she finally managed to gasp, as she handcuffed him. He spluttered breathlessly in response.

He was all run out. That was lucky, May thought. He hadn't enough strength left to resist. She was able to get his hands behind him and click the cuffs on without any help, and without a struggle.

Behind her, she heard the thud of footsteps as Owen arrived.

"You got him, May!" The admiration in his voice gave her a final surge of strength. She'd done it. She'd run down her suspect. Her fitness had paid off, and her determination had been rewarded. He'd been unable to make his getaway. To her surprise, she realized Owen looked intimidated as she stared at him.

For a weird moment, May wondered if this was how her elite, FBI agent sister Kerry felt all the time.

"Why are you chasing me?" Joey finally managed to blurt out.

"You failed to obey an officer of the law. That's a crime. We asked you to stop. You ran. We won't even mention that you were about to drive off in this truck. Because there's something more important than that I need to ask you first."

"What's that?" He was panting for breath, his face shiny with sweat.

"There's been an abduction and a murder in this town. You were seen pursuing and harassing the victim."

"I was?" He looked appalled. "I don't even know who you're talking about! I'm being honest when I tell you this was just coincidence. I meant no harm to anyone. I'm just a friendly guy. Sociable."

May didn't necessarily trust people who told her they were honest. If you were really honest, why would you feel the need to say that?

"We need to know your exact movements," she continued. "When you arrived in town, and what you've been doing on certain specific dates. I hope you can account for your time, because if not, you're a murder suspect. And running from police simply proves that you have something to hide."

He stared at her in a panic, looking cornered.

"I—I didn't do it," he muttered.

"Then why were you trying to flee? Why were you trying to get away from us?"

He looked down and didn't answer. Instead, he swallowed hard. May realized that her words were making the truth sink in. His attempt at escape was not the action of an innocent man.

"We're going to take you in for questioning." Remembering the need for evidence, May added, "But first, we're going to search your tent."

She didn't miss the look of utter dismay that crossed his face as she spoke those words.

CHAPTER SEVEN

May and Owen each held one of Joey's arms as they half-carried him back across the sandy soil. May was very interested to know what they would find inside the tent. Something that Joey didn't want the police knowing about, that was sure.

She hoped that whatever it was, it would get them further with the case. Emily's parents deserved closure, and as soon as possible.

Joey was complaining every step of the way, limping along.

"My legs are aching," he mumbled. "And you're hurting my shoulder."

"It'll hurt more if you keep struggling to get away," May retorted, although she did actually ease her grip on his arm slightly.

"I didn't do anything," he protested, as they reached his tent.

"Then why were you trying to run?"

"I panicked," he said.

"Why were you panicking?" Owen asked.

Joey opened his mouth, but didn't say anything.

May shook her head and wondered what had happened to this man to make him so determined to run.

By the light of her flashlight, she could see that they were almost at the tent.

And then she was startled to see that the beam of the flashlight picked up a figure crouched inside.

May hissed in a breath, stopping in her tracks as she gazed at the clear outline of the shadow.

"Who's that?" she asked.

"Nothing. Nobody," Joey stammered.

Owen kept a tight hold on Joey's arm while May stepped forward.

"This is the police. Come out immediately. If you have a weapon, put it down. Hands in the air."

May waited. Her heart was hammering. What was happening in that tent? Was it a criminal, one of Joey's partners in crime? Did Joey have a victim hidden away in there?

She could hear scuffing sounds from inside the tent. And then the door was hesitantly unzipped.

And out scrambled a schoolgirl.

May heard Owen gasp audibly. Her own heart pounded. A schoolgirl? Captured, held hostage, in the tent?

Even as May's mind leaped to make the connection, she realized there were too many flaws for this theory to pan out. For a start, why would any captured girl have deliberately hidden from sight in the tent, when freedom was just the tug of a zipper away?

And secondly, this was no schoolgirl. Looking more closely, May saw that she was probably in her thirties. Late thirties, most likely. And while the tie and the shirt and the short skirt did look like a school uniform, the same could not be said for those racy stiletto-heeled shoes.

She was a hooker, dressed as a schoolgirl.

"What's going on here?" May asked sternly, looking from Joey to the hooker and back again. The two looked terrified, glancing at each other.

"Nothing," the hooker said, her face white with fear, her wide eyes rimmed with dark liner and mascara.

"Nothing?" May questioned.

"She's just a friend. Just a friend," Joey stammered. "Honest."

"I don't think so," May said firmly.

Owen stepped closer to the tent. Pulling on a pair of gloves, he went inside, and May knew he would be scouring the interior for any signs of contraband, drugs—or any links to Emily, any wood or nails, sleeping pills, anything that might match up with the shocking scene that was etched into her mind.

But it was becoming clear why Joey had been reluctant to have his tent raided, and May was starting to suspect that he'd run for a different reason. He'd run because he'd known his "friend" was stashed away in here, and was worried he'd get into trouble for it.

"I—look, it was just some fun," Joey stammered.

May decided to cut right through the excuses. It was getting late. She needed specific information from him and wanted it now. Then he would either be cleared, or they could bring him in.

"Give me a detailed account of your movements today. And I also need a detailed account of your whereabouts exactly two weeks ago," May said.

Exactly two weeks ago, to the day, Emily had gone missing on her way home from school. So May wanted a clear alibi for that day. And she also wanted to account for what Joey had done today. Had he been near the lake, dumping a body?

She waited. Joey was looking nervously back and forth between her and the hooker, and she realized that he was hoping the hooker would help him out and lie for him. But it was clear from the look on the hooker's face that she was going to say nothing.

May waited. The man was clearly scared. But she had to get the truth from him.

"Look, today I don't really have a clear timeline," he said apologetically. "I did some odd jobs in the morning for the construction guys. They sometimes have extra work for me. They paid me cash and I went into town, got a few things. I, er, I met up with Candyfloss here, and asked her to come around later."

"Candyfloss?" Owen repeated incredulously.

The hooker looked down, shuffling her stiletto-heeled feet.

"Two weeks ago. Can you account for your movements then?" May continued, facing up to Joey.

"Yes. Yes, I can. Two weeks ago, I was out of town for the night."

"Are you sure?" she repeated.

"Yes. I was looking for some spare cash, and a guy at the diner said that there was a camping site that needed cleaning and clearing. It was about four hours from here, up in the mountains. I went with three other guys and we stayed there three days. We worked hard. There was a lot to do. Weeding, tidying, sweeping. He paid all of us cash at the end, and also gave us a ride back here."

"Who was the guy?" May asked.

"I've got his number on my phone. I'll show you now. You're welcome to call him but please don't say anything bad, because he said he might use me again. He paid well." Joey looked at her pleadingly.

"There's no reason for me to do anything but confirm the alibi," May said, reluctantly acknowledging that her own kind heart would not allow her to compromise anyone's chances of getting honest work.

And even though he was definitely an unstable and slightly shady person, he was obviously capable of doing an honest day's work.

Joey nodded and pulled out his phone. He searched through his list of contacts and gave her the number for Howard Harvey, owner of Howard Harvey Campsites.

She noted it down, resolving to call it as soon as possible to confirm this alibi.

At that moment, Owen came out of the tent.

"There's no evidence of any contraband inside," he said.

May turned to Joey.

"Okay. You're cleared. Next time, don't run from the police. It could open you up to further trouble. If you are so innocent, then stand your ground and admit to it," she reprimanded him.

"I will, honestly. I promise I will," he said, looking apologetic.

May turned away. She felt stiff and sore from that chase-down. It had taken every ounce of her strength to catch this man, and he proved to have a solid alibi.

Where were they going to look next? she wondered.

As she climbed tiredly into her car, her phone rang.

"Sheriff Jack?" May answered quickly, thumbing her phone onto speaker so Owen could hear, hoping her boss had some good news.

But it turned out to be the opposite.

"We've just had a report that another high school girl has gone missing," he said. "Her name is Shawna Harding, age eighteen. She was last seen this afternoon, heading out for a run in the forest trails. I'm at the North Forest trailhead now."

May exchanged a horrified glance with Owen.

If this had been called in earlier in the day, she would have hoped that this girl might have simply gone to a friend's, or gotten lost or injured. Now, at after nine-thirty p.m., was there still an innocent reason for her non-appearance at home?

Inside, she feared the worst had happened, and the killer had taken another captive.

"We'll meet you there as soon as we can," she said to Jack.

CHAPTER EIGHT

May gripped the wheel as she and Owen sped through the night, heading for the North Forest trailhead, which was just a few miles out of Chestnut Hill. It was a place she knew well. Usually, she would have thought of this lonely trail, winding its way through scenic forest, as being safe and peaceful, if a little quiet.

Now, she was filled with worry over what might have happened there.

"Surely this can't be a similar incident?" Owen asked, sounding appalled.

"I hope it isn't, and that she is found," May said, not even daring to voice her fears.

But she felt in her bones that the two incidents were connected.

"If there's even a chance that it is connected, then we need to be ready to search for any signs," she said.

They'd been working solidly for more than fourteen hours now, but she didn't feel at all tired as she turned onto the road leading to the trails.

They pulled up at the parking lot where the trailhead was. Sheriff Jack was already there, waiting for them. May saw that a few other cars were also parked there, both police cars and cars belonging to civilians. People were already on the scene.

"Jack," May said. She was distressed to see that his face was lined with worry.

"Thanks for getting here so fast. I just hope we aren't too late," he said. "We've already got search parties combing the two main trails. Do you two want to take the third side path? Mr. Harding is away on business, but Mrs. Harding is coordinating the search and handing out descriptions of her daughter."

"What about vehicles? Are they briefed to look out for her?" May asked, and Jack nodded.

"We've got our patrol vehicles briefed to follow up every lead."

Knowing that this would be hard, May walked up to the start of the trails, where Mrs. Harding was standing near the trailhead with a young man of about sixteen that May guessed was her son.

She was a tall, stern-looking woman who looked as if she might be a no-nonsense businesswoman herself in better times. Now, she looked consumed by worry.

"I can't believe this," she lamented on seeing May. "Shawna said she was going for a run in the afternoon. I asked her where she was headed, just to keep things safe. I never thought anything would happen to her. I realized a couple of hours ago she wasn't home, because she often goes to friends after her run. I called around all her friends. Nobody has seen her."

"What about her phone?" May asked.

"I've called it. It just rings."

"It does?" May said. That was encouraging. At least it was turned on. Perhaps it was still on her person and could be traced.

"Here's a photo of her. I've printed copies," Mrs. Harding sobbed.

Her son silently handed May an eight-by-ten printout of a beautiful young woman, with cascades of chestnut brown curls and smiling blue eyes.

Carefully, May scrutinized the photo, taking in the details. Age: eighteen. Height: five-seven. Weight: approx. 120 pounds. Wearing: Nike running shoes, white. Black running pants. Pink top. Pink baseball cap.

"Thank you for this detail," she said gently to the clearly traumatized mother.

"I hope it helps. I hope something helps. I just can't bear the thought she might—she might be next."

"We will do everything in our power to find her," May promised. "In the meantime, can you tell me if there was anything else happening in Shawna's life?"

"Such as what?"

"Any conflicts, any problems. Any personal issues. Boyfriend issues? Was she having difficulties at school, had she experimented with drugs recently?" May gave as many suggestions as she could, hoping that one of them might lead somewhere.

"No. Nothing like that. She wasn't dating at the moment. She was on good terms with everyone. She was a leader at school, you know. She knew how to stand up for herself. She didn't take any disrespect," Mrs. Harding explained.

"Thank you," May said. "Please, if you do think of anything that could help us, let me know."

"I will," the other woman promised.

36

But as May set out along the trail, she couldn't help but feel heavy-hearted.

The search parties were doing their best, but there was a chance that she had already become the killer's latest victim. May didn't want to think about that. She was determined to be positive, to hope for the best, even if it was against all the odds.

"Shawna," she called, her voice echoing slightly in the stillness of the forest. "Shawna. Can you hear me?"

The silence was eerie. There was no sound to be heard but the rustle of leaves and her own breathing. She paused, listening for any sound that might indicate that Shawna was nearby. There was nothing.

The forest was deeply still.

Her flashlight lit the way among the dark trees. For a few minutes, she could hear the muted sounds of nearby searchers, but then the trails diverged enough that these faded away.

Through a gap in the trees, the moon cast a silvery glow on the trail she was on.

She looked up at the moon, shining high in the sky.

Show me something, she thought. Help me find this girl.

She kept her flashlight trained on the path, hoping that she could pick up footprints, but it had not rained in the past few days and the ground was hard. May saw only the faintest evidence of prints on the forest floor, mere indentations among the dry pine needles and baked soil.

She kept on calling, and so did Owen, but the only answers were the distant calls from other searchers farther along the trails.

"I think I see something here," Owen, who was searching on the other side of the trail, said.

May veered in that direction.

"Look here. It's faint, but visible. Shoe prints. Heavier ones, as if someone was running. You can see them here, where there's some loose sand on the trail."

"Are there two sets?" May crouched down, peering at the ground, wishing that these tracks were clearer, because between the hard ground and the thin sand, no actual tread was visible.

"Yes, I think so. Two sets."

May took a look at the distance. The footprints indicated that people had been running, fast.

She turned to Owen.

The first set were consistent with a jogger's stride. The second set looked longer. The stride was several inches longer. Someone was running, and the stride was longer to accommodate them.

And then, from ahead, she heard a loud musical tune.

Owen and her stared at each other.

"What was that?" he asked incredulously.

"A phone?"

They rushed forward, sprinting along the track. May barely noticed the ache in her legs.

There it was. A bright screen, half-buried in the foliage near the edge of the trail. The tune was repeating over and over.

May peered down at the screen.

With a sinking of her heart, she saw it read "Mom."

Mrs. Harding was calling her daughter's phone again, and this time, May had found it, abandoned and fallen, close to a place where two sets of footprints indicated a pursuit.

This was telling a chillingly accurate account.

May had a strange feeling. It was as if she was being watched. She couldn't see anybody, but a cold chill ran down her back.

"Let's take a look around and see if we can find anything else that could help us," she said.

Carefully, they worked their way through the undergrowth that had been allowed to grow long alongside the path. May didn't know what she was looking for. Any other trace of evidence. Something discarded by the monster who had grabbed this young woman as she ran.

But even though she looked carefully, shining her flashlight into the shrubs and weeds, she saw nothing.

"Let's take the phone back, at least," she acknowledged, feeling defeated, even though they had found a very important piece of evidence.

Owen reached into his pocket, taking out a glove. Carefully, he picked up the phone.

"I guess we'd better take this back now?" he said.

"I guess we'd better," May replied.

This was, without a doubt, a serial crime that was centered on kidnapping and abduction. And given this, she knew what her boss would decide to do.

It was time to go back and face up to her fears, and hear Sheriff Jack say the words she dreaded.

CHAPTER NINE

"We're going to have to call in the FBI," Jack said to May, who cringed inwardly, knowing she'd been right. At least she'd expected it.

He handed the phone to one of the officers, who took it back to the vehicle they were using. The scene was still busy, but people were wrapping up now. The floodlights were being switched off and the search parties returning. The phone being found meant that Shawna was nowhere nearby, and that she had been abducted. A sense of defeat hung in the air.

The problem, May knew, was that calling in the FBI meant they would send a local agent. And that meant her sister would arrive. Having her sister involved in a local case would be a hugely complicating factor. She knew this from experience. Not only did it add multiple levels of stress, but May found it emotionally hard when Kerry, who loved the limelight, commandeered a case involving May's own local community. It brought all her demons to the surface, the demons that told her she was not good enough, inadequate, and a lesser investigator than Kerry was.

Giving herself a stern talking-to, she told herself that Kerry's presence might help, and if it did May would be forever grateful.

But she knew that her sister's interference might also complicate the case and create an extra element of tension that May surely could do without at this pressured time.

She really didn't want this, but she also saw how her boss had no choice. There was no indication who the perpetrator was. This was summer, when there was an influx of people in the area. Undoubtedly, the first victim had been held for a while before she was killed and it was likely the same might happen to the second.

That abandoned phone. The ringing seemed to echo in May's ears. Such a forlorn and terrible sound. Shawna's mother had unlocked the phone, but there was nothing on it that had been helpful. No suspicious calls or messages. No photos taken by Shawna before her disappearance.

Whatever resources were available—whatever they could do to try and track down the man holding the missing girl—would be welcomed.

And May knew that the FBI had far more resources than their small local police department could rustle up. So it was better to put her personal angst aside and accept that this was the right call. She'd have to deal with the stress. At least, after a lifetime of living with Kerry, she was used to it.

"I agree we could use more help," she said. And then, getting it out of the way since it was obvious, she continued, "My sister is local. We could contact head office, ask for help, and suggest they send her?"

"Exactly what I was thinking." Jack sounded relieved, and May wondered if somewhere down the line, her perceptive boss had sensed the rivalry between her and Kerry. "I will call them and ask if she can come out. Hopefully, that will give us a big head start tomorrow."

May acknowledged that it was now well after ten p.m. She'd been at work at six-thirty a.m. to open up. Owen had arrived at seven. They'd had a day filled with shocks, and a challenging chase-down included.

There was nothing more they could do tonight but wait, even though it felt excruciating to do so when a new victim was missing.

"Shall we go have a drink?" Owen asked.

May guessed that would mean going to Dan's Bar, which was their local watering hole. But surprisingly, she found herself okay with the idea of it. Two months ago, the thought of going into the bar would have had her in a cold sweat of anxiety as she wondered if she'd get the courage to speak to her crush, Dan.

But now, May was realizing that she was stronger than the idea of an unspoken crush. She wasn't quite at the stage of thinking she was over this crush, but she thought that time might be in sight.

If Dan didn't say anything flirty, or actively ask her out, May guessed there was hope that she could possibly go to that bar and behave like a normal person.

And tired as they were, she didn't think Owen's invitation was anything but genuine. They were both done with today. The idea of a date was not on the cards. Both of them were now in survival mode, needing to refuel and rehydrate.

May felt totally comfortable with this.

"A drink is a great idea. Maybe a burger," she said.

"I'll buy the burgers," Owen volunteered.

"I'll buy the drinks," May then said.

With this sorted out, they climbed into May's car and she drove tiredly toward the town center of Fairshore.

Fifteen minutes later, they walked into the glamorous interior of Dan's Bar, which was just a couple of blocks away from the police department.

The crowd was thinning out at this late hour, but there were still a few people who were finishing up their drinks, and one or two others who looked to be glued to their seats for the night, or until Dan kicked them out.

May and Owen took the last two seats at the bar, and Dan himself came to take their order.

"Hey, May."

She sensed that he was making a huge effort not to ask about Kerry. It was only recently that she'd realized Dan had a huge crush on her sister. Since Kerry had recently gotten engaged, Dan had exuded a faint aura of hurt whenever she was around him.

He was exuding it now.

"Two beers, please," May said.

"And two burgers, please, with fries," Owen added.

May was glad about the fries. She hadn't wanted to seem greedy by asking for them, but she was starving after the long day. This was just one of the ways she and Owen seemed to be in tune. It was almost as if they had read each other's mind.

May sat back in her chair, relaxing a little, enjoying the sounds of the eighties hits on the jukebox.

But the fact she and Owen were so in tune made May even more undecided about what decision she should make about the dating. If the topic was even open for discussion at all.

Dan handed back their drinks.

"Cheers," Owen said.

"Cheers." May clinked her glass against his.

She liked the way he was looking at her. The small lines around his eyes made him look kind, and his brown eyes were gentle.

May felt a surge of affection for Owen. He'd been a great friend since day one. He didn't interrupt her daydreams—he didn't even make any. He was a quiet presence in her life. A support.

The kind of man she could see herself with if she was to get married again. Unlike the drastic temper tantrums that had entered their marital home during her first short-lived marriage.

But how was she even thinking of that topic? May felt stunned it had entered her mind. And as if tuning into her—again—Owen asked, "Your sister, Kerry. How's the wedding prep going?"

Dragging her focus back to the question, May said, "It's been demanding. Kerry wants everything to be perfect all the time. Including, and especially, her wedding. So we're all trying hard to get it that way."

"I'm sure she'll have everything she wants," Owen said with a wry smile that told her he understood her predicament.

"Kerry always gets her goals," May agreed.

Dan brought the burgers, which looked like the last word in deliciousness. Tall, sumptuous, with thick, browned patties, rich cheese, and just the right amount of pickles and lettuce.

Grabbing a fry and the salt shaker, May felt her mouth water. Time to replenish all the calories she'd spent chasing down Joey.

"I can imagine Kerry always gets what she aims for." Owen frowned in concentration as he added ketchup to his fries. "But are you okay? Is she pulling you into the preparations that much?"

"I'm okay," May said. "I'm happy to help. She's my sister, and she's getting married to a great guy. I want the best for her. I just feel a bit torn in two."

She knew—and Owen knew—she was talking about her job and her commitments to her career.

May took a bite of her burger, glad of the distraction. She trusted Owen but all the same she didn't want to reveal too many of her personal thoughts. Not even to herself, May realized. They were not easy ideas to confront, and in the battle between family loyalty and her dedication to her job, there was also no simple answer.

The burger was delicious. May ate fast and hungrily. She knew that after such a long day, within a few minutes after eating the food, her body would be demanding some shut-eye. With such a pressured case on the go, she needed all the rest she could get in the next few hours.

At that moment, May's phone beeped.

Checking it, she saw a message from Kerry.

"Hey sis! Your boss just called. Sounds like you've got an urgent case down there. No wonder you need my help! I've booked on the 5 am flight tomorrow. I'll be landing at 6 am. Not sure if the rental agencies will be open so early. Small town, you know? Can you pick me up?"

May sighed.

She should have known that having Kerry flying into town would upend her life all over again. But she was right. At that hour, the local rental agencies might not be open, and every second counted in this case.

She took a moment to devour the last bite of burger, and scoop up a forkful of salty fries, before replying.

"Sure. I'll be there."

Downing the final gulp of her beer, May tried to make peace with the fact Kerry would be working with her on the case.

It was not a competition, she reminded herself, even though the girls had grown up in a super-competitive environment thanks to her mother, a schoolteacher, who'd pitted them against each other constantly.

This was not that time, May knew. They needed to work together to solve this.

But she couldn't help hoping that her own efforts would not be overshadowed by the might of the FBI, and that she would be able to contribute to the case to ensure its success.

She feared that it would be taken away from her, and that she would feel, all over again, that she was not good enough to help solve a crime that was devastating her own community. May knew that even though Kerry was going to want to manage this case, she needed to stand up for herself and not let her steamroll over her ideas.

If this crime was committed by a local, then her own local knowledge would be critical to solve it. In fact, May was convinced that this would hold the key. This killer knew the area. He knew the old boathouse and the quietest trails. He'd been able to work in secrecy.

Thinking about it, May was becoming more and more sure that this killer was no stranger and no drifter, but rather somebody from the local community.

First thing tomorrow, May decided, she was going to do her own research on the potential suspects, use her local knowledge, and make a shortlist of people who had links to both these victims.

CHAPTER TEN

Shawna gasped in horror as the cabin door swung open. She'd been alone for hours in this secluded room, with only a wooden stool and a few thick blankets inside. The adjoining door led to a tiny outhouse, with a toilet and basin, but there was no window or door there. Just a tiny ventilation gap in the log wall. She knew it was in the middle of nowhere, because she'd screamed and called for help until she had no voice left.

She had battered her fists against the thick wooden door, but there was no means of escape.

Now, there he was, the man who'd chased her down. The man she knew was going to kill her. She jumped to her feet, cringing back against the wall, ready for his attack.

But he was strangely calm as he opened the door, stepping quickly in before locking it again.

"It's okay. It's all okay, don't be scared," he soothed her in the same gentle voice that she remembered, as she stared in shock. "I'm not going to hurt you, I promise."

He held out a hand that was shaking slightly.

In it, she saw a candy bar.

"Would you like it, perhaps? Or a drink of water? Did you see that there's a bathroom and toilet to the side of this room? The water there is clean and drinkable. There's no hot water, I'm afraid, but I put soap there for you if you need it. But perhaps you prefer bottled water?"

Anxiously, he produced a water bottle from the bag he was carrying. It was icy cold; she could see condensation on the sides.

"I'm not going to hurt you," he said again.

He sounded so anxious, so upset. But he was holding her prisoner. He was a stalker and a kidnapper. And he was going to kill her, she thought with a renewed sense of panic.

"Let me go," she entreated him. "Please, let me out of here."

"I can't do that."

She gasped. "You can't? Why not? What are you going to do with me?"

She could see his shoulders hunch at her question. He took a deep breath.

"I'm not going to hurt you. I want to keep you safe. You might not believe me, and I can see you are very frightened, but you need to trust me. Just now, we'll have a little talk and then you'll understand more."

He stared at her, and she saw a weird, fake warmth in his eyes.

"Please, have some water. I don't want you to be thirsty." He unscrewed the cap and offered the bottle.

She took a small sip, as if from a poisoned chalice. She was so thirsty, and her throat was like sandpaper from screaming.

"Please don't hurt me," she breathed.

"I won't hurt you," he promised.

She took a few more sips. She'd almost forgotten that she was so dehydrated. She was also very hungry. Her stomach rumbled loudly, despite her fright.

He gave her the candy bar.

"Please eat. I know it's been a long time since you had food. I don't want you to be hungry, or uncomfortable in any way. Later on, I can bring you some hot chocolate. It's made with real chocolate. Sweet and good."

She felt confused by how he was babbling on. Why was he saying these things? Frowning, she took the candy bar, but didn't unwrap it. Perhaps she'd eat it later. More importantly than food, she needed a way out of this place. It felt as if the water she'd just drunk had replenished the energy and resolve she needed.

"Thank you," she whispered.

She felt hope. Maybe, just maybe, this man wouldn't kill her. Maybe she could get out.

"I need you to do something for me, please," he then said.

Frightened again, Shawna stared at him.

"What? What must I do?"

"Take off your shirt," he asked calmly.

"No!" She recoiled, dropping the bottle. "No, I won't do that!"

"It's okay. I promise I won't look. But I have to have you put this one on."

He held out a different shirt. It was a small, blue school top and she could see immediately it was a couple sizes too small for her.

"But that one's too small."

"It's okay. I promise." He sounded so reassuring. His voice was soft, coaxing. "Please. Do this for me."

He looked worried and upset, as if he had no choice but to ask, as if he had no other options.

She took the top with shaking hands.

She stared at him, thinking of her choices. There weren't many and she didn't like any of them.

Give in, and do what he wanted? Or refuse to do as he asked? Then he might hurt her, despite what he'd said.

She didn't want to do it. She was embarrassed, and this was all getting weirder and weirder.

But then he turned his back, just like he'd promised her he would.

She decided she might as well do it. Then maybe he would let her go. Quickly she pulled her dirty, sweaty pink top over her head. She put on the one he handed her, which was clean and ironed and smelled of fabric softener.

Shawna's hands were shaking so bad she struggled with the buttons. One flew off. And she heard the underarm seam give way with a ripping sound.

What was going on? Why did she have to wear this strange, too-small shirt?

"Are you done?" he asked.

"I'm done," she said.

He turned to look at her again and saw her standing there with the shirt not only on, but buttoned up.

Could she get past him? Shawna eyed the door. Where did that lead?

"You look lovely," he said. "Just lovely."

He was being so sickeningly caring. She had no idea why he was doing this. What were his reasons for giving her all this fake sympathy and treating her like some kind of a doll, while making it very clear she was his prisoner?

She was trying to weigh her chances. Of getting out, and of what he'd do if he caught her.

The door was only a few feet away. Beyond, it was dark, and she had no idea where she was. Was it the middle of the night? Was he alone here, or were there other people around?

She wished she knew where she was. It was very quiet. She couldn't hear any other sounds.

Perhaps it was a house? Had he brought her to his home? But he'd told her there was no hot water, so what kind of house didn't have that? More likely it was a cabin, a hunting cabin, something similar.

She had no idea how long she'd been here, but she thought they'd driven for at least half an hour to get here. She'd been tied up in the back of his truck and blindfolded, but he'd gone over the bumpy roads gently. Carefully.

So what were her chances of getting out of here and finding help?

"You're looking at the door," he said, sounding worried again.

Shawna looked away.

"You don't need to be afraid. I'm not going to hurt you. I'm going to do what we need to do soon, but you mustn't be scared. Promise me. There's no reason to be scared at all. I mean you no harm."

He closed the door softly and her heart thudded. She'd lost her chance to get away. She heard the key turn in the lock.

She was still a prisoner. If there was another chance—any chance at all—Shawna resolved she was going to take it.

Otherwise, she knew, this fake, overly kind man was going to kill her.

Of course he was. She didn't believe a word he'd said. He meant her harm, and she knew it.

CHAPTER ELEVEN

Arriving at the local airport terminal next morning for the pickup, May felt stressed and worried. She'd had a sleepless night thinking about Shawna, wondering where she was, if she was still alive, what was happening to her. She'd been worrying about making her shortlist of suspects, deciding on the best starting points she could use as soon as she'd done the airport run and was at her desk in the police department.

May narrowed her reddened eyes as she pulled up outside the arrivals department, seeing that Kerry was already waiting there.

She'd wanted to be early, to get there first, and in fact she had arrived early. But it seemed Kerry's flight had landed even earlier.

Her sister looked every inch the successful FBI agent. Her short, blond hair was perfectly cut in a pixie style. Her expensive leather jacket and black cargo pants hugged her slim figure, making her look both gorgeous and intimidating at once.

Next to her stood the man May recognized from the last time as her case partner. Tall, young, and full of himself, Special Agent Adams was staring around the airport in a confident, superior way, as if he'd bought shares in it. He ran a hand over his dark hair, which had been sharply cut, and adjusted the lapel of his navy blazer.

"Morning, sis!"

Kerry grabbed the door as soon as May stopped, climbing in the passenger seat. Adams opened the trunk, stowed their bags, and got in the back.

"Morning, Kerry. Morning, Adams," May said, noticing her voice sounded hoarse and grainy. After the stressful day yesterday and a stressful night, she felt worryingly short on sleep.

Glancing at her sister's left hand, she saw the diamond engagement ring sparkling in the morning sun.

"May, I'm looking forward to this," Adams said in the back. "I'm keen to help out the locals."

"What a disturbing case! Quite similar to the last one we were involved in here, in that both sets of victims are being abducted and held. It's actually a crime trend we're noticing is on the rise, especially in these rural areas."

"It's very helpful to be tapping into the trends. Gave us a big advantage in our last case," Adams said.

"It did. It allowed us to solve it within a very fast time. Who knows why these cases are proliferating out of town. Social pressure, the economy, or simply that there's more inefficient policing in the outlying areas." Kerry, too, was full of conversation as she fastened her seatbelt. "Not here, of course," she added hurriedly.

May took a moment to study her sister. Her blue eyes were bright and alert, and she looked ready to take on anything.

"It's good you're here," May said, pulling away.

She decided to be positive and ignore what might have been a veiled insult, but was more likely Kerry's mouth running ahead of her brain as she sought to remind everyone in the car why she was so indispensable to the case. Getting offended would not be helpful or allow them to solve the case any faster, May told herself.

"I was reading through the notes last night," Kerry added. "Getting a full picture of what we have here."

"Very complex," Adams interjected from the back. "Good thing you called us in."

"I'm just worried about Shawna," May said. "What if she's still alive? We've got to find her."

"We're on it. You and your team have the FBI's full support on this." Kerry's tone was firm and confident.

"Where do you want to start?" May asked. "I thought it would be a good idea to make a shortlist of contacts. Do you want my help with that?"

"Well, actually, I'm going to start with the strong suspect I've already identified," Kerry said, sounding smug. "And, by the way, we also have to look in on our parents at some stage, but we can get to that during the day."

"What?" May stared at her in shock, not even taking in what Kerry said about their parents. The car swerved slightly and she corrected it hastily, focusing her attention once more on the road. "You already have a suspect?"

"Yes," Kerry said. She was clearly keeping her cards close to her chest.

"Well, that's great news," May said, still confused by the speed with which this had played out. She waited for Kerry to tell more, but when she didn't speak, May was unable to stop herself from asking, "So what's the lead you've uncovered, then?"

"I'm not sure I can share it." Now Kerry sounded cagey.

"And why can't you share it?"

"It does involve confidential information," she said thoughtfully.

"What do you mean?" May said, seething. She'd obviously been assigned the role of chauffeur, while Kerry and Adams got down to dealing with the case. "We're on the same side! What information do you have that you think is so confidential it can't be shared?"

And how, exactly, had Kerry gotten hold of this strong lead within hours?

"It involves something I'm not sure I'm at liberty to discuss," Kerry added.

"We are not at liberty," Adams reminded her from the back seat, rubbing it in that he knew what it was, too.

"What?" May asked, even more frustrated now. "Can you just tell me?"

"She just told you," Adams said from the back seat. "It involves confidential information. We're not allowed to discuss details."

Kerry smirked. "You see, it does involve sealed juvenile records," she said.

"Oh," May said. She knew that the FBI could access some of those, which again was not possible for a local deputy. Again, the circumstances they were operating in were very different.

"So, you have a suspect. And you're going to track him down?" she tried, looking for another angle that might work. "You don't think that as the local deputy who's managing this case, I need to know every step?"

"May, it's our case, and we're going to cooperate on it, of course. You are here to provide any local knowledge that I haven't already been able to obtain. But please understand, I have to lead the investigation."

May felt herself seething again at the note of quiet arrogance in Kerry's voice.

"Is that it, then?" she said in a near-accusatory tone.

But then she took a deep, calming breath, knowing she needed to stay focused. Kerry was right. The FBI was the one with all the resources, and they were the ones who'd be expected to solve the case quickly. She was just the sidekick. She sighed.

"Absolutely. You're in charge," she agreed, not wanting to fight over this seemingly petty, yet somehow important, fact.

As if Kerry was also willing to give a little now that May had reinforced she was in charge, she smiled.

"I guess I can tell you, seeing we'll be driving there together. Because we do need to go straight there."

"Where do I head?"

May had just reached the highway. She glanced at Kerry, who was consulting her phone's maps.

"Take the turnoff for Chestnut Hill and then turn right."

"Is this the suspected killer? Or someone with information?"

Kerry checked her watch. It was only just after seven a.m.

"He should be still home," she said in satisfied tones, without answering May's question.

"Who?" May asked, now feeling consumed by curiosity.

"He's a potential killer, for sure," she admitted.

"Why? What's his motive?"

"He has a connection with both victims, and a strong motive for wanting Emily dead."

"Both victims? Kerry, c'mon. Who is this person?"

May felt ashamed by how much like an eight-year-old baby sister she sounded in that moment. Kerry had the knack of doing that to her, stringing her along, and much as May tried to resist, she inevitably ended up behaving the same way. Kerry had done the same as far back as May could remember. It was May's fault, she knew, for falling back into that role.

But luckily, Kerry seemed unable to keep the information to herself a minute more.

"When I saw the case details, I immediately went and did some intensive research. I looked into the backgrounds of other people at the school. Seeing both Shawna and Emily went to the same school, it was the first place to look for a common thread."

"And did you find anyone?"

"Yes, I did. A guy named Callum McGee."

"Why do you think he's a suspect?"

Taking the turnoff for Chestnut Hill, May glanced at Kerry as she stopped at a light. Kerry was looking quietly satisfied.

"He's an ex-boyfriend of Emily Hobbs and Shawna Harding. I checked their social media for the links and information. He's quite the school celeb. He's the captain of the football team and also plays for his state. He's on the athletics team, too. But he has a sealed arrest record."

"Which you unsealed?"

Kerry nodded mysteriously.

"And?"

"He faced charges of assault last year, at the age of seventeen. Charges which were filed by Shawna Harding, his girlfriend at the time."

May's eyes widened in excitement. "That does sound promising."

Kerry nodded, looking pleased and determined.

"He has links to both the victims. He has actual charges against him that were filed by one of them. The charges were dropped, but I'm not sure why that happened. It could well be that the reasons for the victim dropping the charges are somehow related to the reasons for the crime."

"That would make sense," May said.

"Kerry's a genius at research," Adams said, sounding satisfied.

"Thank you," she replied. "Anyhow, he's going to be our first stop. You see, local knowledge also works from afar, when you have the right resources."

"Yes, I see that," May said humbly.

"Turn left here," she directed May. "Callum's house should be the second one on the right, going up the hill. If he can't give us clear answers and a strong alibi, we might just have our suspect in custody in a few minutes. Hopefully, he can then tell us where Shawna is being held."

CHAPTER TWELVE

May was filled with equal parts admiration and envy for Kerry, as she drove up the hill and parked outside the second house on the right. This was the suspect's house. A strong suspect. Callum McGee had a juvenile assault record, and a history of involvement with both victims.

Imagine if this crime could be solved within the hour. Imagine if Callum was able to give the whereabouts of Shawna Harding, and she could be returned safely to her family?

That would be a huge result. It would all be down to Kerry, whose brilliant investigative mind had discovered the crucial details at unprecedented speed. She'd be the hero of the hour.

However, May felt consumed by worry that people would think she, as the local deputy, had done a poor job. After all, she hadn't yet explored any shared romantic interests between the two girls. That was because the second victim had only been taken last night, and in comparison with the FBI, obtaining information locally was slower. By the time they were done with the search for Shawna, it had been too late to go and interview anyone from Chestnut Hill High, or have a look at who was who in the school. May had been planning on compiling her shortlist first thing today and she'd anticipated the research would take a few hours.

But regardless of the reasons and excuses, the truth was that Kerry would have cracked the case effortlessly, and May worried how that would sit with the locals. Would they still trust her as their county deputy, knowing that it had taken an outsider to come up with the fact that a local boy was their killer? She tried to calm her fears by telling herself firmly that as long as the case was solved, that was the main thing. If the killer was caught, lives would be saved, and that was what mattered most.

May took a look at the house as she climbed out of the car. It was an older house, and didn't seem well maintained.

For a homely, friendly town like Chestnut Hill, it wasn't really the sort of place that you'd imagine the popular high school football star living in. Dust had settled on the veranda. The garden was overgrown and the mailbox was sagging at an odd angle, leaning against the fence like it was about to fall. In contrast, the home next door, separated by a solid brick wall, looked perfectly maintained, making this house seem like an even bigger eyesore.

"It's a dump," Kerry said. "That could be because Mr. McGee is divorced. I read that in the police report. He's divorced, and his son lives with him."

"Clearly, neither father nor son are house proud," Adams said. "It's a pity. A blight in such a picturesque area. You know how quaint I've always thought this community to be."

"I think you have mentioned it in the past," May mumbled, which was a nicer way of saying Adams had used the word "quaint" several times an hour, and in a deprecating way, while driving around Tamarack County.

"Let's go speak to him," Kerry said, leading the way up the uneven garden path.

May and Adams followed her up the path to the front door. Glancing to her right, May noticed a small workshop. That was something to keep in mind, she thought, thinking of that homemade raft. If there was any woodworking being done in there, it might be worth seeing what it was.

"Callum McGee?" Kerry called, knocking on the door.

It was opened by an older man who May guessed must be Callum's father. He had bushy, graying hair, a narrow face, and a suspicious expression.

"Yes?" he said in a deep voice.

May noticed a shotgun propped by the door. Beyond, the hallway was lined with trophy animal heads. A musty smell wafted out to meet them.

"Good morning, sir," Kerry greeted him. "My name is Kerry Moore and I'm an FBI agent. We need to have a word with Callum, if he's here?"

"What's this about?" He glared at them, eyes narrowed. "My son's here, but he needs to go to school. Come back later."

Beyond him, May saw a tall young man standing in the corridor. He was a good-looking, athletic man, with broad shoulders and dark hair. However, he had the same suspicious expression on his face that May could see on his father's.

"I'm going to have to ask you to let us speak to your son now," Kerry said, gently but firmly, as though she were speaking to a class of unruly children.

"Tell me why, or I'm not letting you in."

"It's in connection with the recent crimes. The murder of Emily Hobbs and the abduction of Shawna Harding."

"What? My boy is not involved in any crimes. What are you even harassing us for?" He sounded outraged.

"Sir, we just need to speak to Callum to get a few details," Kerry said, her tone still pleasant.

May was impressed by how level Kerry could keep her voice. She herself wondered why the father was being so defensive. Was he protecting his son? Was Kerry's theory one hundred percent right?

"I'm not harassing you," she added. "You can be there the whole time. I just want to ask him some questions." She gave a pleasant, yet steely, smile.

With an angry sigh, the man capitulated. He stood aside and Kerry marched into the dusty-smelling home. Callum watched them warily. He didn't look pleased to see them inside at all. May thought he looked nervous and shifty.

"Callum?" she asked. "Where can we speak?"

"Come in the kitchen." Mr. McGee gestured to a door at the far end of the short corridor.

They headed into an untidy kitchen. With five of them in there, the space felt crowded.

Kerry sat down at one of the four seats around the wooden table, gesturing for Callum to sit opposite. May and Adams stood either side of the door to the corridor. Callum's dad stood threateningly at the head of the table, looming over them.

"I'd like to ask you about your past relationships, Callum. I understand you have dated both Emily and Shawna."

"No, not really," Callum said reflexively, running a hand through his thick, dark hair.

They were only just in the house, and he'd already lied. The air of tension in the kitchen seemed to thicken.

"We have some questions about your relationship with Shawna. About what happened between you."

"Nothing happened. Shawna blew it out of all proportion. She had no right to do what she did."

"Why do you say that?"

Callum didn't answer Kerry, but stared at the table.

"When did you break up?" Kerry then pressured him.

"We broke up months ago. What has any of this got to do with that murder?"

55

"Callum," Kerry said, and May could hear her patience wearing thin, "I am going to ask you the questions. Not the other way around. Now, what happened during the break-up?"

"Nothing. We had a big fight. I didn't harm her. We were both angry. She acted way out of line."

What was he talking about? May wondered.

"What are you talking about?" Kerry asked.

"This is about those trumped-up charges, isn't it? They were dropped," Mr. McGee said menacingly. "My boy's no criminal. Sure, he was angry with her. She should never have done what she did afterward. But that's not our problem anymore."

May felt instinctively that in this home environment, they were going to get no further answers. Mr. McGee felt the need to dominate on this turf, and the son was taking his lead from his father.

Kerry was obviously thinking along the same lines.

"I think you'll have to come in," she said. "We need to question you in more detail at the police department."

Callum looked flabbergasted.

"You think I'm a murderer." It was a statement, not a question. And he said it as if he couldn't believe it.

He looked horrified.

"My son wouldn't do anything like that!" Mr. McGee said. "I want to protest this harassment. I know my rights. I'm going to see you people in court."

"We have every right to detain your son for questioning."

Kerry stood up. And then, to May's shock, Callum did, too. He made a dash for the door.

May lunged forward, grabbing his arm firmly. It was like hanging onto a steel piston. This football player was strong! In fact, he nearly dragged her right off her feet.

And, the next second, Callum's father weighed in on the fight.

He leaped forward, fists swinging wildly as he aimed a torrent of angry blows at May.

It was so unexpected, and she had both her hands so tight around Callum's arm, that one of the punches caught her on the ear and she staggered back, falling over a broom that she hadn't seen in the corner of the kitchen. She landed painfully on her backside in a sprawl of limbs, with her ear ringing from the blow.

"It's okay!"

Adams jumped to the rescue, leaping forward and grabbing the father's thrashing fists. He expertly got him up against the wall, with a hand twisted up behind his back.

In the meantime, Kerry had moved lightning fast to grab Callum's hands behind his back. She didn't seem as surprised by his strength as May had been, because the click of handcuffs sounded in May's ears as she was still untangling herself from the broom and scrambling up from the floor.

With her face burning, May felt as if she'd been completely shown up by these two expert FBI agents. To her shame, she realized she'd been, in that moment, the clumsy, bumbling amateur of the group with her ill-timed fall.

Adams was muttering threats in the father's ear.

"You're not beyond suspicion yourself, sir. We're bringing you in, too. We're going to hold you for now, while I search the premises."

"Good idea," Kerry said, as Adams cuffed the father. "Let's get these two guys into custody, and you stay behind and do a thorough search of the house, Adams. Pay particular attention to that workshop."

She sounded pleased, as if she felt the investigation was getting somewhere.

May trailed behind as Adams and Kerry hustled the father and son out to the waiting police car and bundled them inside.

"I'll keep a watch on them. You drive," Kerry told her.

Feeling as if she was nothing more than a chauffeur and not deserving of any police status, May set off for the Chestnut Hill police department.

She hoped she would have a chance to redeem herself during the interrogation, because so far, she'd proven ineffectual. Worse still, she'd embarrassed herself in front of two people who she knew wouldn't forget in a hurry.

CHAPTER THIRTEEN

May trailed behind as Kerry strode into the interview room at the Chestnut Hill police department. She still felt mortified at what had played out earlier, and how ineptly she'd acted in the moment. How humiliating that had been.

Adams was still searching the house, and when he'd finished, Owen was going to go and pick him up and bring him to the police department. There, the two of them would watch from the observation room. Kerry had decreed that May could join her for the questioning.

"You have local knowledge, too, after all," she'd said kindly.

Personally, May couldn't wait for Owen to join her. He was the one with the real local policing knowledge. And she needed moral support. She felt very much on the back foot here.

Her ear was still sore from the blow, her backside felt bruised, and she didn't think that either of the McGees looked cooperative at all. Walking in, she saw that Callum was sitting next to his father, and she could see the family resemblance in their identical glares.

"Okay," Kerry said briskly. "Gentlemen, I'm sorry I had to bring you in, but we have to have full answers to our questions, and at your house, I wasn't getting them. Resisting an officer of the law unfortunately counted against you also, but at least it gave us cause to search your premises. Now, we're going to allow you to sit together for now, but if we get further trouble from either of you, you'll be separated and we'll question you individually."

She smiled at them smugly.

"You're wasting your time again," Callum scowled, but then he raised his eyes to May. "Besides, what are you doing here anyway? You're the local sheriff. Isn't this an FBI case?"

May had to stop herself from gasping aloud at that low blow.

Kerry gave him a quick, hard smile.

"FBI always cooperates with local police. Boots on the ground, you know? But anyway, we're here to discuss you, not her. And I'd like to start by knowing more about your movements yesterday. We're going to get straight on to how you accounted for your time, and if you can't account for your time, you will be facing criminal charges."

"I refuse to answer until I get a lawyer," Callum said.

May had no doubt he and his father had been discussing this before they walked in.

"Your movements yesterday," Kerry threatened.

"Not saying," Callum snapped back.

May decided to intervene.

"Were you at school?" she asked. "I know you go to Chestnut Hill High. Were you there yesterday? If you were, you can say. You won't get into trouble for it."

"Yes, I was," he said angrily.

"How do you get to school? Do you cycle? I think I've waved to you on your bike," May said, memory suddenly helping her. Now she knew who the dark-haired man was that she'd seen on her patrols, whizzing through the school gates, usually late.

"I ride a bike, yes," he agreed, clearly surprised by May's personal knowledge of him, and remembering her wave.

Now Kerry was looking at her, astounded.

"So are you saying you cycled to school yesterday?" She quickly took over.

"Yes, I did."

"And then home again?"

"Yes. I cycled home too."

"What time did you arrive at school?" Kerry asked.

"After eight," Callum said.

"Can anyone confirm that? Was there roll call? Did you go straight to class?"

"I don't understand. Why do you want to know?"

"Just answer the questions, please, Callum," Kerry said.

"I got to school at about quarter past eight. I had History. We had a test in that class. I didn't go straight to class. I went down to the locker room to get something I'd forgotten."

"What did you forget?"

"My notebook."

Kerry raised her perfectly groomed brows, as if assessing this answer.

"What time do you remember leaving school?"

"About ten past three. I remember because I looked at my watch."

"And did you go home right away?"

Now Callum's face darkened again. "I don't have to answer."

"What time did you arrive home?"

"I've told you enough," he snapped. "I don't have to tell you any more."

59

"Do you ever use your dad's car? I see it's a pickup. There's a good amount of trunk space there. Did you use it yesterday?"

"Not answering!" That question had struck home. His face was flushed red now, May saw.

"Tell me about your history with Shawna. Why did she file charges against you?"

"I won't answer that. It was totally unfair!"

May realized they were getting back to the same situation they'd been at the beginning. And they didn't yet have enough information to clear Callum in terms of his movements. The fact he was not willing to answer readily was definitely counting against him, she thought. Unfortunately, the window of time that remained outside of his school hours would have made it possible for him to grab Shawna.

And he wasn't answering! Why not? What was he hiding?

"You've bullied my boy enough," his father blustered. "He is not the killer. It's totally obvious."

Kerry now turned to him.

"We also need to piece together your movements. Where were you yesterday morning and yesterday afternoon, Mr. McGee? Can anyone confirm your whereabouts?"

"I won't allow this!" Mr. McGee shouted. "We are both being wrongfully accused here. Go find someone who's really guilty. I will not be bullied or trapped into answering, and I know how you police like to twist things. I demand we call our lawyer. Now. Before we say another word!"

May exchanged a glance with Kerry.

"Let's step outside," Kerry murmured.

May followed her out. Kerry closed the door behind her and then leaned back against it and exhaled slowly.

"He's being very obstructive," she said.

"He is," May agreed.

Kerry nodded. "It's highly suspicious that neither of them will properly account for their time. But we need more information. We don't have enough yet."

She sounded frustrated and May felt a surprising flash of sympathy. It was easy to forget, when up against Kerry's competitive personality, that deep down she had her own insecurities.

"We have to have something that can link him to the crime scene. There's got to be something linking him to it all," May said.

Kerry checked her phone.

"I see Adams has just messaged," she said, sounding hopeful. She opened it and read the text. Then she made a disappointed face.

"No people in the home. No trace of anyone being held or imprisoned. The workshop is used for metalwork. They make wine racks, wrought-iron shelves, and the like. No evidence of woodworking. Owen has arrived there and they're on their way here."

May sighed.

For a despondent moment, they stood together in silence. May felt deeply worried that they had the right person in the room, but that they were not going to be able to prove it. This could stall the case. It could be disastrous.

"I suppose we could go back in and try again," Kerry said after a moment.

"I don't think they'll say anything," May said.

"We'll see," Kerry said, but her voice sounded grim. Then she glanced at her watch. "Actually, I think we have to let them stew for a while. Mr. McGee is too defensive now. He needs some time to cool down and start regretting his actions. Maybe he'll realize how much money the lawyer will cost him. Then we'll go back and try again."

May nodded. She knew they couldn't give up yet. Even if he did insist on a lawyer, they could still go back in when the lawyer arrived. Perhaps the lawyer would encourage Mr. McGee to be more reasonable. He couldn't actually make him any less reasonable, May acknowledged.

At that moment, Adams and Owen walked in and May felt her heart give a flip-flop of relief as she saw her tall deputy arrive.

"Morning, May," Owen said cheerfully.

"Morning, Owen," she replied, feeling like she might actually want to smile for the first time that day.

Adams looked less pleased.

"I wish we'd found some evidence in the house or the workshop. But there was nothing. I couldn't find anything. No woodworking equipment. No sign of anything that could have been used to subdue or sedate the victims, and no sign of anyone being held there. There was barely even a lockable door in the place," he said.

Kerry stared at him, and May thought she looked frustrated.

"It seems to me that we're stalled for now. We're going to have to wait until this lawyer arrives because the McGees are simply refusing to talk."

"You've tried everything?" Adams asked, frowning.

With her lips pressed together, Kerry nodded.

"Even that technique you used to break Menzies in that case a while ago? I mean, he was a criminal kingpin and he crumbled, right?"

"I didn't get far with that at all. It didn't work with these two."

"You want me to go in and speak to them?"

"They are firmly refusing to say a thing till they get their lawyer," Kerry insisted. "It's a waste of time going in there. But I don't know how long this lawyer will take to get here. We need to think of another direction to pursue this in the meantime."

They were quiet for a moment, all staring at each other despondently.

Then Owen cleared his throat.

"You could always interview Mrs. McGee," he suggested in a helpful voice.

"Mrs. McGee? Did you not hear what I said earlier?" Kerry said, sounding irritated.

"He wasn't there," Adams said.

"Oh, yes, that's right. You weren't there. The McGees are divorced, and Callum lives with his father. So speaking to the mother might not be very helpful." Kerry tossed her head disparagingly.

"I think it will be," Owen insisted. "After all, she lives in the house next door."

"What?" Kerry and Adams swung around, uttering the word in unison as they stared at him. May felt a flash of pride.

"How did you know that?" Kerry demanded.

"I saw her looking over the wall when I was waiting for Adams. She was interested to know why someone was prowling around her ex-husband's workshop. I gave her a few details. She seemed to be happy to speak quite openly to me, so I said that the FBI might be back soon to ask for more information."

"Well!" Kerry exclaimed.

"From what she told me while we were chatting, they co-owned the property so they divided it up when they divorced. I also picked up that they don't like each other much. But they are in each other's business, a lot. So I think if you go and speak to Mrs. McGee, she might be willing to tell you more," Owen advised with a smile.

CHAPTER FOURTEEN

He'd left the door open.

Shawna struggled with the soft ropes tying her. He'd tightened them so carefully. Considerately. Mumbling apologies to her the whole time. As if he was politely trying to get past her in a crowded nightclub, not actually tying her up with rope.

It was creepy and terrifying. She'd been numb with terror.

He'd locked the door before he started so she hadn't had a chance to escape. She had been imprisoned in that small, wooden room. But after she was tied, he'd left it open.

Shawna yanked her hands up as hard as she could.

He'd tied her tight, and before he left, he'd smoothed her hair down and assured her that he'd be back. That he wasn't leaving her.

That was exactly what she was afraid of. That he would be back.

Shawna pulled as hard as she could. She had to get out of the ropes that held her. She had to get out of here.

She braced her elbows against the floor and pushed up, trying to wrench the loops looser. And thanks to how ultra-considerately he'd fastened them, it worked. There was some give. Enough for her to drag one of her hands out of the knotted ties.

With a rush of relief, she freed the other. Her hands were shaking, but at least she was no longer a prisoner.

The knots on her ankles were easy to undo now. Shawna crept to the door and looked out.

He was out there, down the track. It was far enough away that she couldn't see him. She could hear him, though. He was working with wood. Sawing, cutting, drilling.

The sounds filled her with fear, because they brought to mind that he was somehow going to hurt her. That whatever he was doing or making was intended for her.

She wasn't going to stick around to find out.

Tiptoeing along, Shawna headed down the path.

She didn't know what was beyond the house. She didn't know if there was anything. She was deep in the woods and she didn't dare go near where she thought he was now. She needed to find another way out of here. No matter what it took, she had to.

She tiptoed down the track.

Her feet scrunched over the sandy surface. It was early morning, and the trees pressed darkly against the path, lining it impenetrably. If she didn't take the route to the lake, there was only one way to go, and it was this way. She thought it led down to a road, because she could hear the sound of a car speeding past.

Just one car, then silence again. This was not a busy road, but she had to get there. Get away from that maniac.

Hurry, Shawna.

The trees on either side of the drive crowded in on her, blocking her way. Breathing roughly, Shawna stumbled forward, her heart pounding.

The gravel was skittering under her feet.

She couldn't tell where she was, or which direction would be closer to civilization. It was all unfamiliar, and so remote. It felt like the middle of nowhere.

Feeling as exposed as if she were running down a street naked, Shawna hurried down to the blacktop road. Surely, once on the street, she would be able to get help.

Shawna ran, feeling the grit of the earthen track scrape her shoes. If he caught her, she wouldn't be able to run away. Don't think of that. Just run. Run. Run.

Her head was spinning. She felt weak with fear.

Keep going. Don't look back. Her breath came in ragged gasps.

Keep going.

She could see the road now. It was a dark line, bisecting the space in front of her. Her feet hit the blacktop and it was smooth and level. No more skidding and stumbling. But where were the houses? Where were the people who could help her? This really was in the middle of nowhere, in the early, gray dawn.

"Help!" she screamed. "Help me!"

Her shouts made her throat hurt. She was so hoarse that she couldn't get enough sound out. And she had a chilling feeling that there was nobody around to hear her anyway.

Instead, she needed to put some distance between herself and this creep. She decided to turn right.

Shawna ran, her breath rasping in her throat. The too-small shirt was constricting. Her chest felt tight. Her arms couldn't move enough. Her feet slapped along the road. One-two, one-two. A memory came into her mind of her taunting another girl to run, just the same way, when Shawna had caught up with her after school.

That girl had been younger and weaker and she'd ended up crying. Shawna had laughed at her plight. She'd told herself that the strong survived and the weak deserved it. But now she was the weak one, and she was realizing just how scary it felt.

Behind her, she heard a growling noise.

Her heart accelerated. What was it? Was it an animal? For all she knew, something could be chasing her, or lurking in the woods.

But then reality cut through the haze of fear that was surrounding her. Of course it was no animal.

It was a car!

Shawna saw the glare of headlights in the gray predawn behind her. Someone was driving up behind her. She was safe. She could be saved now.

The car drew closer. A battered-looking pickup. It must belong to a local.

"Help me!" she yelled. "Help me!" She turned to the car and waved her arms. Relief flooded through her. She was safe, she could get out of this nightmare and away from this psycho who had grabbed her.

But to her surprise, the car didn't pull up beside her and stop. Nor did it speed ahead and ignore her.

She felt the distance closing between her and the car, more slowly than she'd expected. But then it simply drove a couple of yards behind her.

Tracking her.

Stumbling, Shawna turned, gasping in concern, trying to see past the headlights, which were on high beam, past that battered hood, and inside the tinted windshield.

She couldn't see enough, but she was starting to fear.

Gasping in a sob of air, she turned and stumbled on, glancing to the side, but the road was lined by two deep ditches. There were only sheer banks falling away to the left and right. There was no access point, no convenient path where she could dart out of the road, and in any case, it was light enough now that she couldn't melt into the darkness.

She was starting to realize who was behind her, driving so patiently, so slowly. There was no one else it could be. With a coldness in her stomach, she understood that this was just another part of the hunt for him. That he'd always been confident he would find her.

Then she let out a scream as she heard him call out to her.

"It's okay," he said. "I'm here, Shawna."

His voice sounded gentle. It was so calm, so reassuring.

"Go away!" she screamed.

"Now, Shawna. It will be easier if you do this of your own free will," he chided her. "Don't make me have to get out and run after you. Because I will do that, if you feel like running for longer."

Heaving for breath, Shawna wavered and stuttered to a stop. Her hands on her thighs, she struggled to catch her breath. He wasn't going to give up, no matter what. And he'd proved before he could outrun her.

She collapsed to the ground, covering her head with her hands. There was no point in running now. She was so tired.

He stopped, and glancing up, she saw him roll down the window.

Now she could see his expression. He looked so concerned.

Tears started to stream down her face. She was trapped, and she'd been so close to being free.

"Now, now," he said. "I'm here now, Shawna. I'm here to help you. I don't mind that you ran. I'm just glad I found you, so we can have our talk."

She needed to run. She had to get away, but she couldn't. She had no strength left. This had been her last attempt. He'd known and he'd seen and he had followed her from the time she'd left. There was nowhere she could go. And nobody to hear if she screamed.

He was getting out of the car now. She saw his shadow move.

He appeared at her side and crouched down.

"It's okay. I just didn't want to scare you. I could hear you screaming for help. I came as fast as I could."

She saw him smile. And she saw his hand reach out, and he touched her on the shoulder.

"Don't worry," he said. "Everything's going to be fine."

CHAPTER FIFTEEN

May sped back to Callum's house, with Kerry in the passenger seat, feeling eager and anxious to interview Callum's mother. Thank goodness for Owen and his local knowledge, which had allowed them to take this next step.

Hopefully they would make progress with this next interview. May felt sure that Mrs. McGee would be able to tell them something that would bring them closer to the truth.

As Kerry drove, her phone started ringing.

"Well, look at this. It's Mom on the line," she said, sounding happy. She switched the phone to speaker and picked up the call.

"Hey, Mom!"

"Hey, Kerry!" May heard her mother's delighted tones resound around the car. "Are you here in Fairshore?"

"Not in Fairshore at the moment. We're nearby, though, in Chestnut Hill."

"Who's we? You and that wonderful young, dynamic investigation partner of yours?"

"No, Mom. It's me and May. Say hi!" Kerry waved the phone in May's direction.

"Hi, Mom," May said, sounding as enthusiastic as she could.

"How lovely to think of you two sisters together!" Her mother sounded genuinely pleased. "I must say, this case has really traumatized the neighborhood. I've had a few people asking me what May's doing about it and if there's any hope in sight. I told them not to worry, that they're bringing Kerry in, and that it will all be sorted out soon."

May felt shame overwhelm her. She didn't think her mother even noticed how humiliating her words were. She was so used to thinking of Kerry as her golden daughter, the one who was not just talented but had actual superpowers.

"We're working together," Kerry said kindly.

"That's wonderful. Of course you are. When you're wrapped up, I need to see you. We have so many wedding details to discuss. Do you think you'll be done by dinnertime?"

"We're hoping so," Kerry said.

"Then come for dinner. I'll make us something special. Roast lamb, perhaps?"

"Sounds good, Mom."

"And May, you're invited too, of course! I'm sure you're eager to discuss a few wedding ideas."

"Absolutely." May felt her stomach twist. She didn't know how much more of this conversation she could take. Luckily they were now turning into the road where the McGees lived.

"I'll touch base with you later, Mom. Got to go now. We're gathering information. Hopefully, we'll have made an arrest by lunch time."

"That's my daughter!" Mrs. Moore's voice rang with pride. "Let me not keep you. Good luck, not that you need it! Take care!" She cut the call.

May stopped outside the house and they climbed out. Putting that nerve-shredding parental conversation aside, May was able to focus on the home. This time, she saw how the dividing wall did, in fact, bisect the large property. The one on the left was in a state of dilapidation. The one on the right looked newly built and as neat as a pin.

They walked to the shiny, green-painted front door.

Kerry knocked first and then rang the doorbell. There was no response.

"Is she at work? She doesn't seem to be in," she said.

But at that moment, May spied movement in the back yard beyond the house.

"She's there. Look! Mrs. McGee?" she called.

A slim, redheaded woman was bent over a flower bed, wearing gardening gloves and wielding a trowel.

She glanced around at them and then put the trowel down and walked over, taking off her gloves. Her face was as good-natured as her ex-husband's was surly.

"Mrs. McGee, we're from the police," May said.

"Yes, I was expecting you. The deputy I spoke to earlier said you might come by."

She stared at them curiously.

"Your ex-husband and son were taken in for questioning," Kerry said, summarizing the sequence of events.

"And did they give you answers?" the woman asked.

"They are not being very cooperative so far, ma'am," May admitted.

"Well, that's no surprise, given the debacle that played out with that poor girl a few months ago. I love my son, but if he and his father have one thing in common, it's a complete inability to handle problems and conflict in a constructive way."

May felt encouraged. It definitely sounded as if the mother would be willing to fill in the details.

"Are you aware of what happened? I believe that there were assault charges laid against your son, but they were dropped. It all sounds complex and sensitive," May said, returning her focus to the matter at hand.

Mrs. McGee sighed. "You'd better come in," she said, glancing at the street outside as if she didn't want the neighbors seeing her speaking to the police in public.

May walked into a home that looked immaculate and smelled fresh and clean. It was furnished in gray, blue, and white. There was a new-looking television in the cabinet, and a vase of fresh flowers was on the coffee table.

"I'm sure you can see we're very different people," Mrs. McGee explained. "We're amicable now, but I still wouldn't say we're friendly, and I won't do unpaid labor for him either, so his house doesn't get cleaned."

They followed Mrs. McGee into the living room and sat down on a neat leather sofa.

"We need to get to the core of these assault charges. Do you know what happened?" May asked.

Mrs. McGee nodded. "What happened was that Callum did something idiotic. In fact, he and Shawna both did. It was a few months ago. Not long before his eighteenth birthday."

"What was that?" Kerry asked.

"Callum took some shots of Shawna while they dated. In her underwear, posing like a Victoria's Secret model, or so he said. I never saw them. But when they broke up, they fought very badly. Both of them were vicious and said horrible things to each other. And as a result of that, Callum threatened that he was going to take those photos and circulate them to all his friends."

May's eyes widened. "Oh dear."

"Yes. Shawna was off-the-scales angry about that. She was furious, and I don't blame her for that. It was idiotic of my son to make that threat. Anyway, Shawna went to the Chestnut Hill police department and she filed a charge of assault."

"And Callum got arrested?"

"Callum got arrested. Then we all got involved in trying to manage the situation before it exploded way out of control."

"What happened in the end?"

"In the end, both sides lawyered up. Callum agreed to apologize in writing and sign an affidavit that he would delete the photos and would not share them. And she agreed to drop the charges, which she did."

"And was Shawna happy with the outcome?"

Mrs. McGee shrugged. "That, I'm not sure. I don't think she was. I think there was more to it. Something more was said, or threatened, or done after that. But I never found out what it was. My ex-husband refused to tell me."

May raised her eyebrows. She could understand why, after having had that play out, neither the father nor the son had wanted to speak out about the assault charges. She could see now that they both had a strong motive for wanting to silence Shawna, if she had not been happy with the apology and had wanted to escalate the situation further.

"My son is not a killer," Mrs. McGee said firmly, as if reading May's mind. "He's made bad decisions and done stupid things, but he is not a murderer."

"And his father?" Kerry asked.

She shrugged. "I don't know what he'd be capable of, but I have to say I would not expect he could do such a thing. And to be honest, Shawna was no angel either," Mrs. McGee said.

"What is your impression of her?" Kerry asked. May could see she was fascinated by this information. She was leaning forward, looking curious and focused on the other woman's words.

"Please, this must be off the record," Mrs. McGee said. "She's a missing person, and I do not want to speak badly of her in this small town."

"It will be off the record," Kerry promised.

Mrs. McGee sighed.

"She's a beautiful girl. And a good student. But she's a bully. She takes advantage of weakness. She's a very hard, brutal person for one so young, and I'm sorry that my son ever got involved with her."

May felt her eyes widening. Mrs. McGee had spoken with real resentment in her voice.

"Is that so?" Kerry asked.

"Yes, it is. Thanks to her, my son has a criminal record that will stay with him for life. And as I said, although she dropped those charges, I think she tried hard to make sure that was not the last of it."

"Thank you for that information," May said. "And what about Emily? I know Callum dated her a while back?"

Mrs. McGee nodded.

"Emily wanted to get back together with him recently, I believe. But I am not sure if Callum wanted to do the same. Things between those two were very complex. It was also a rather destructive relationship. He still has to find the right person for him, but he keeps choosing women who aren't."

"That's very helpful," Kerry said.

May felt encouraged after this interview. It put the focus firmly back on the father and son again. Lawyer or not, they now had a lot more ammunition for their second round of questioning the McGees, and she hoped that it would allow them to get to the truth.

CHAPTER SIXTEEN

May felt determined to get past the McGees' resistance as they sped back to the police department. She was sure Kerry felt as confident about this new information as she did.

For once, she actually felt in harmony with Kerry as they climbed out of the car and strode into the department.

"We're going to get them this time. You watch," Kerry said.

"The McGees' lawyer arrived about ten minutes ago," the deputy at the desk said, sounding apologetic. "I let him go through."

"That's fine," Kerry said.

They stepped into the small interview room, where May was immediately hit by a powerful wave of cologne emanating from the resolute-looking young lawyer who was sitting next to Mr. McGee.

His dark hair was gelled back, he had gold rings on four of his fingers, and he stared at May and Kerry with absolutely no warmth whatsoever.

"You need to release my clients now!" he thundered. "They are innocent of this crime!"

May was unimpressed. She was sure Kerry was too.

"I'm sure everything will become clear soon," Kerry said calmly.

"You can't hold them indefinitely," the lawyer said. "Not without evidence. They're innocent until proven guilty."

"So long as a crime has been committed, we will do what is necessary to ensure the safety of our community," Kerry said. "Murder is a very serious allegation. We need your clients to answer some questions."

The lawyer glared at her. "I will use every resource I have to protect my clients. I trust you have some evidence that supports your accusations?"

"We certainly have discovered this case is a lot more complex than we thought." Kerry stared at him smugly. "Nobody in this room has so far mentioned that Shawna Harding filed assault charges against Callum because he threatened to make public some revealing photos of her during their break-up. Perhaps you handled that issue? I believe lawyers got involved on both sides? And I believe that there were also further issues that arose after the charges were dropped?"

May saw Callum's face turn brick red. The young lawyer shifted uncomfortably in his chair. "I don't believe that is of interest to you," he said.

"If it was not of interest, you wouldn't be here," Kerry said, with a smirk.

"I want them released," he demanded. "There are no grounds to hold my clients with regards to that matter."

"We are just beginning to collect evidence. This is only the first day of our investigation. The point is, both the McGees have real motive and opportunity for this crime, and we need to talk about that." Kerry sounded calm but firm.

"That matter is irrelevant," the lawyer insisted.

"It's very relevant," Kerry said. "We all know now that Shawna was a very, very angry young woman. She filed charges. She was seeking further revenge or recourse. And now she's missing. To further complicate things, Emily, the girlfriend who wanted to get back together with Callum, but he didn't feel the same way about her, is dead."

The lawyer looked startled by the amount of information Kerry possessed. He was clearly beginning to feel uncomfortable.

"I will not have my clients intimidated," he demanded, but May thought he was actually talking about himself.

She felt like someone watching a tennis match, her attention swinging from Kerry to the lawyer. She didn't feel ready to offer anything useful. With a feeling of admiration, but inferiority, she decided to stay in the background.

"What played out after Shawna dropped the charges?" Kerry pressured.

"Nothing that is relevant," the lawyer insisted.

"Tell me, or I will hold them here for as long as it takes."

"You haven't filed formal charges!" The lawyer was getting louder now.

"Oh, but we can," Kerry said, with a grim smile.

"You can't do this to them! It's not fair! Callum is part of a state football team. You're going to damage the career of a promising young athlete by exposing him to reputational harm!" he said, looking more and more desperate.

"We're only trying to find out the truth," Kerry said.

May felt impressed. She was staring at Kerry, who looked like a different person in that moment.

But the lawyer was silent.

Suddenly, May thought she knew what the missing piece of the puzzle was.

She cleared her throat.

"Did the McGees give Shawna a payout?" she asked the lawyer. "That's what it seems like to me. I guess she wasn't happy and she demanded reparation for her emotional pain and suffering. Did you pay her out in a private settlement deal?"

Three shocked faces turned in her direction. Actually, when Kerry swung around to stare at her, May counted a fourth.

"Er," the lawyer said. "It's not relevant."

"It would make sense, right?" May said. "And perhaps you were angry about having to do that, or worried she might ask for more money down the line?"

That would be a clear motive for murder, she thought.

There was a long, uncomfortable silence.

Kerry smiled. "Bank statements, please. I'd like the McGees' bank statements for the past six months. From all their accounts, and I will check up on that. Providing full bank statements is going to be one of the conditions of their release from being detained by us. Of course, it will be pointless if you can't provide the other conditions."

"And those are?" the lawyer asked nervously.

"Alibis," Kerry said firmly. "If you have them, we need them. If not, I'm afraid charges are in your clients' future. The immediate future."

"How can you do this to innocent citizens?" he demanded, looking from Kerry to May.

"We can," Kerry said, looking very serious. "Your clients are both now suspects in a criminal investigation. They don't have many rights at the moment. If they want to stop being suspects, then help us to find the real killer before any more people get hurt."

"Look, they have alibis. They do. I can give you the details, but I must ask for a guarantee of privacy."

"Why's that?" Kerry asked.

"Because unfortunately, both alibis for yesterday afternoon involve activities that are somewhat irregular," he said.

"You can't go telling her!" Mr. McGee blustered.

"I have to," the lawyer said apologetically.

"Fire away," Kerry challenged.

"Callum was at a bar the whole of yesterday afternoon, in Southridge. I know he's underage. He went drinking with a friend, Michael Evans, who will confirm the alibi if needed. The barman will recognize him and can confirm he was there. Callum used his father's car and I believe there are cameras outside the bar to prove this."

The lawyer sighed.

"And where was his father while this played out?" Kerry asked.

"Mr. McGee was in the next street, visiting with a close friend. He was with her all afternoon. Her husband was out of town for the day. They do have proof, in that some photos were taken. These I have, with the time stamps on the phone."

The lawyer stared expressionlessly at Kerry. Mr. McGee stared at the floor.

"We'll check the alibis," Kerry said. "I'll look at the photos too. If these are genuine, and you provide the bank statements, then you can have your clients back."

She smiled at the lawyer. "I'm sorry if we've caused any inconvenience," she said.

"We're innocent," Callum blurted out. "You're looking in the wrong direction. If you ask me, you should be talking to my team manager."

"Your team manager?" May asked, surprised.

"Mr. Jessop. He's the manager for the sponsored junior and young adult state teams. He knows both the missing girls. He's the one who didn't want them around me. In fact, I saw Emily get into the car with him on the afternoon she disappeared. It was at the sports ground where the state team does the training. She climbed into his Mercedes there."

Having delivered his bombshell, he stared at them defiantly.

CHAPTER SEVENTEEN

Chanel South trailed out of the school grounds. It was eleven thirty a.m. At this hour, only bullies and losers got sent home. It was a Chestnut Hill policy that bullies got kicked out of the school grounds, but only after they'd been ignored for long enough to make sure they caused damage.

She was not a bully, but with the bruise on her cheek, she sure looked like one who had gotten into a fight.

And if she was a loser, then so what? Nobody wanted to have anything to do with losers. She felt sore, stiff, and angry, mostly at herself.

"I didn't get into a fight," she muttered to herself. "I was attacked. And what I did was self-defense."

She'd been defending her younger sister, actually. Because at this school, bullying was a problem. Chanel had been able to keep her head down, but Briony, her younger sister, was taking the brunt of it.

Chanel was not a popular girl. She didn't have many friends, but that was a choice she made.

She'd once been popular. At the end of primary school she'd been part of the group that ruled the school, and could have continued to occupy a place of respect in middle school. But Chanel had made a decision to cut her ties with that group, and with the girl who led it.

The way Chanel saw it, she'd made a clean break. She'd never felt the need to hang out with them again.

But she'd felt the need to stop that group from harassing and hurting Briony. Chanel had moved on; Briony hadn't. The bully was now picking on Briony.

Like a lioness protecting a cub, Chanel had muscled in to stop one of the girls in the clique from bullying her baby sis.

And she'd suffered for it. The girls had ganged up on her. She had the bruise and scratch marks on her neck, and she'd taken a few punches to the head and arms also.

She ached, not only from the assault, but from the fact she'd been sent home while they got off free and clear.

"And they're going to be talking about this all day, getting more and more popular because they beat me up."

She had to go home and deal with the shame, and she was sure it wasn't going to be a pretty picture. Chanel hated this school. She hated these girls. She hated her parents for making her come here. How was it fair that she was getting punished for being a good sister?

She trudged along the street, her head down, concentrating on her shoes and her feet, putting one foot in front of the other, not thinking about much else.

Her father would be in the middle of a work day, so he wouldn't be around to calm Mom down and keep her from blaming Chanel for the whole thing. Her mother would probably believe whatever the other girls told her. She was a real cheerleader for whatever the popular girls did.

And home was a long way off. Five miles. A long walk in the summer heat. Usually, she took the school bus or her mom fetched her. But having been kicked out, she had no choice but to walk. The alternative would have been to call her mom, but Chanel hadn't wanted to make her mad.

But things had to get better. She was through taking this crap. She had decided to make a stand, to stop things once and for all. To stop being a victim. She needed to take a stand and call out the bullies. The fact that they were basically running the school was unacceptable. And picking on innocent people like her baby sister was just mean. It must be stopped.

Now she just needed to work out how to get it done.

Her legs ached as she set off up the hill, conscious of her torn sleeve and her bruise and her messy hair.

And then she heard a car slow down behind her. She glanced around.

"Hey there," a man said, leaning out the window and calling in her direction. "You okay? You need help? Or a ride?"

She stared, a little suspicious. "I'm fine," she said.

He looked like a normal guy, though, she realized. Not some weirdo. Just a plain, normal guy in a biggish pickup.

"You sure? I could take you home if you need me to."

She paused. She hadn't expected him to offer her a ride, and it seemed so reasonable, she hated to refuse.

"No, it's okay, thanks."

"You look like you're having some problems."

"I just have to get home." She turned away, staring at the hill, which felt as insurmountable as her problems.

After this, the bullies were going to home in on her more than ever.

"You been fighting?" he asked sympathetically.

Chanel shrugged. "Guess so," she said.

She wasn't going to tell him she'd been beaten up. And yet she felt an urge to talk to him. It was probably because he was a stranger, and he seemed to understand the way she felt.

But she didn't want to admit being weak. That a bunch of girls had gotten the better of her and that while she'd saved her sister, she'd been the one who'd taken the brunt of the blame.

"Get in. I'll give you a ride. I'm going to an appointment that I'm early for, so as long as you're not more than a few miles from here it won't be a problem. I had a daughter at your school so they know me. I'm not a stranger."

She wasn't sure it was a good idea. Her parents would go nuts if they found out she'd been getting rides from strangers. But then, they'd go nuts if they found out she'd been sent home, so she was in trouble regardless. She glanced at her wristwatch. It was going to take ages to get home now.

A ride was better than a long, hot walk.

"Get in. It's not right to walk around looking this messed up, you'll get people worried."

She hesitated as she stared at the empty road ahead of her. "I guess," she said.

"You want a soda? I brought one for my daughter, but you're welcome to it," he said.

He rummaged in a bag and handed her the can. It felt icy cold in her hand.

"Thanks," she said.

Perhaps she was being an idiot not to take this ride, since he'd offered her a drink and was being kind. And he was a local, it wasn't like he wasn't from around here. She could see from his car's number plate, and the stickers in the back window. He was local.

She sipped the soda and felt a lot better. It was cold and sweet, and made her face feel cooler. And it was a long way home.

"Okay, thanks," she said. "I'll take a ride."

He opened the door for her. Chanel hesitated once more.

Something inside her was whispering a warning. That this was too convenient, the guy was too nice. Other girls had disappeared recently, although they had clearly been grabbed off the street by a predator or psycho, and not by a normal citizen like this guy was.

Even so, if she hadn't been so hurt and battered by the events of the morning, she might have thought again.

But as it was, she didn't think things could get much worse than they already were.

The car was cool, with the AC blasting. Music was playing. Music she liked.

Without thinking too much more, she got in and closed the door.

CHAPTER EIGHTEEN

May saw that Kerry was as excited as she was about this new lead. If Mr. Jessop, the team manager, was genuinely linked to both the victims, this would surely mean they had their killer.

The question was how they were going to prove it.

"We each have a job to do," Kerry decided, when they convened in the police department's back office. "I'm going to base myself here, go into the FBI databases and do some groundwork, finding out more about this team manager and his links to the victims. Adams will check the bank statements to make sure the McGees were telling the truth about that payout. And you and Owen could go and check the camera records at the sports center to see if we can pick up footage of Emily Hobbs getting into that car."

"I think that's a great idea," May said.

She felt relieved that she would be getting out with her feet on the ground. And amped that once again, she could partner up with Owen.

Owen, too, looked eager to be setting out on this mission.

"Explain to me again," he said as soon as he got in the car. "Who is Mr. Jessop? I didn't overhear all of that last interview with the McGees."

"He manages a few of the biggest sponsored junior and young adult football teams. According to Callum, he had interactions with both Shawna and Emily in the past couple of weeks. Callum said the last time he saw Emily, she was getting into a car with him."

"That's significant. Do you think he's some kind of a predator? I mean, being involved with junior teams would give him a lot of opportunities if he was that kind of person."

"I don't know. But we first need to check the footage, and then we need to question Mr. Jessop about it. Something definitely seems irregular here."

"It does," Owen agreed.

May turned onto the main road that led to the sports center, which was a communal sports ground situated between three towns, Fairshore being one and Chestnut Hill being another.

The sports center was a large building with a big, paved parking lot and very extensive facilities. It had three football fields, a gym, an athletics track, basketball courts, and tennis courts, as well as various other sports facilities and fields.

May parked outside. Even though it was still morning, and a school day, the place was busy. A lot of schools bused their students here, she saw. There were two buses in the parking lot, and several students waiting outside the main entrance.

All were engrossed in their phones.

May saw that there were cameras along the building's front wall, which she felt glad to see. She headed inside to speak to someone who could organize access to the footage.

A middle-aged woman sat behind the reception desk. She was speaking on the phone as they walked in, but disconnected the call soon after.

"Can I help you, Deputies?" she asked, nodding a greeting.

May thought she seemed like a competent and efficient type, and clearly a sports lover, with her outdoors tan and her graying hair cut in a short, chic style that reminded May of Kerry's.

"We need to view your camera footage, please," May said.

The woman raised her eyebrows.

"Is this in connection with that strange murder?" she asked, sounding horrified. "I know Emily came here a couple of times with her school. Is there a chance her killer was here? We're already getting calls from parents, asking if it's safe for their children to be here alone."

"We're following up on some information that may be connected to the crime," May said, not wanting the town's grapevine to buzz any more than it was already doing until they had confirmed what they were looking for. "But it is definitely worthwhile for everyone to be more aware of safety. Please remind students they should only get into a car with their parents," May said, feeling the warning couldn't hurt.

The receptionist gave her a curious look as if hoping she'd reveal what she meant by that, but May wasn't willing to say more.

"You are welcome to search the footage," the receptionist then said. "We keep records in the back office. Let me take you through there and show you how to work it."

She got up and headed across the reception room to a small office on the far side.

Inside, it was semi-dark, with blinds covering the small window and several computer monitors on the wall.

"To access the records, simply click Archives. The footage is saved by date, so each day has a different folder. We keep it for thirty days," she explained.

"Thank you," May said.

She and Owen sat down on the chairs and as soon as the receptionist had left, they went hunting.

"Here's the date that Emily went missing," May said, finding it in the archives. "She went missing in the early afternoon. I'm going to see if Kerry's found any information on Jessop's vehicles so far."

She checked her messages.

Sure enough, Kerry's first stop must have been the car details, knowing that May and Owen would need them. May read her text.

"Jessop drives a black Merc most of the time, registration below. Two outstanding speeding fines. Also owns a few other cars that he uses mainly for out of town trips and supercar conventions. Descriptions and registrations below."

"Afternoon, black Mercedes. Let's go back and look," Owen said.

Owen scrolled back through the footage, while they both scanned the moving images, looking for any sign of the relevant vehicle.

"Is that one? No, sorry, that's a BMW," May said.

Owen kept scrolling. They had another false alarm when a black Lexus pulled up. May's stomach was churning. She couldn't believe that this intricate teamwork might lead them to the moment when they saw the killer—the actual killer—take his victim. Had it happened at all? Was Callum telling the truth? And if so, what had played out on this sunny afternoon two weeks ago, but what felt like a lifetime ago?

And then they both said, "Stop" at the same time as the car they wanted came into view.

"That's it. A black Mercedes."

Sleek and shiny, it was clearly a new and expensive vehicle. The driver got out, and May had her first view of the slightly grainy footage of Jessop as he strode inside. She was sure by now, Kerry would have texted her a whole selection of clearer photos of the suspect, but for the moment, this was enough.

He was a tall, dark-haired man who carried himself with authority. In a black suit jacket and chinos, he looked every inch the sporty businessman that one would expect to manage a successful state team. May thought he looked arrogant, but admitted to herself that she couldn't see clearly enough to be sure.

"How long do you think he spent inside?" she asked. "Was he meeting with the team or what?"

"I guess a team meeting would take, what, half an hour? Maybe longer, if he was also doing assessments on the athletes," Owen hazarded.

He pressed the fast-forward button again, but almost immediately drew in a sharp breath.

"There! Look!"

The time stamp showed that just ten minutes later, Jessop was walking out with a young woman following a short distance behind him.

Without a doubt, this was Emily, and May drew in her breath as she saw Jessop open the door for her. She climbed into the passenger seat, and Jessop got in the driver's side.

Then the car sped off.

May looked at Owen in amazement.

"She went with him? Just like that?"

"Did she know him? She must have known him if she came there for school events. And if she'd dated Callum, I guess she might have met him. I mean, she followed him out!" Owen agreed.

"That timing doesn't make sense," May said. He had been in and out too quickly for a meeting, surely.

"Well, it does, if you think about what his reason for going there must have been," Owen pointed out.

"He came there to get her. That must have been the reason. He walked in to find her, he found her, and he went out to the car with her."

"And that was on the day she disappeared," Owen agreed.

May thought this was highly significant. In fact, she was getting cold chills.

Owen clicked on the replay button, so they could watch the footage over again. They both stared in silence as the scene played out a second time.

"I think we have our suspect," May confirmed.

"Where will he be now? At work? Does he have offices?" Owen asked.

"I've been hearing my phone buzz a few times. I think Kerry's sent more info through," May said, quickly reading the incoming texts.

"Yes. He does have offices, and they are just down the road from this sports center," May said.

"We need to go there immediately. I hope he's in," Owen said.

"He has some serious questions to answer," May agreed.

She strode out of the sports center, nodding a thank you to the receptionist, and then she and Owen ran for the car.

CHAPTER NINETEEN

Two minutes later, feeling breathless, May pulled up outside Jessop's offices. She stared at the imposing building where even now, she hoped their suspect was waiting for them.

Did he have any idea they were on his trail? May wondered. She hoped not. She didn't want him to take any last-minute evasive action, or do anything to compromise the progress they were finally making.

"Wow," Owen said to her, as they got out of the car and looked up at the sleek, modern, three-story building that was clad in glass, with steel detail. "Must be a lot of money in kids' sports."

"Yes, I think at state level, sponsored football is big business," May agreed.

They parked behind a security boom that was opened for them by a guard. The first thing May noticed, because she was looking out for it, was the sleek black Mercedes, parked in the bay closest to the building. That was an encouraging sign, although it made her nervous as well as excited to see it there.

They climbed out and then walked up the five wide stairs to the large entrance.

They went in through automatic doors and found themselves in a reception area. Extravagantly decorated in designer style, and with a marble reception desk and chrome detailing, it looked more like a five-star hotel than an office.

The blond receptionist looked as if she might be a part-time model. She stared at them, surprised, when they walked in.

"Can I help you?" she asked.

"Deputies Moore and Lovell," May said. "We're looking for Mr. Jessop."

The glance she gave the elevator immediately gave away that he was upstairs.

"Do you have an appointment?" the receptionist asked.

"No, we don't," May said.

"Er, I need to check he's not in a meeting." She smiled apologetically. "If it's about a sponsorship deal, you will need to speak to the relevant person in our marketing department." For a moment, she sounded as if she was on autopilot.

"This is urgent police business," May reminded her politely, showing her badge to make up for being in plainclothes today.

The blonde blushed. "Oh my goodness," she said, looking worried. "Of course. My apologies. You did say you were deputies. I'm sure Mr. Jessop will see you. Please take a seat and I'll let him know you are here."

She got on the phone and spoke in a quiet voice.

After a short conversation, she nodded and hung up.

"He's just finishing off a meeting, and he will see you in his private office. It's on the top floor, at the end of the corridor. You can wait there for him."

"Thank you," May said.

They walked to the elevators and stepped into the mirrored car, lush with a thick green carpet.

It rode smoothly up, and when the doors whooshed open, May saw a marble-tiled corridor stretching to a large wooden door at the end. They walked along it. May knocked, and when there was no answer, she pushed the door open. Butterflies were fluttering inside her.

The office was enormous, with a gigantic oak desk, a large boardroom table, two leather sofas, a shelf lined with trophies, and a photo wall that was covered in framed shots of key moments during matches, trophy ceremonies, and team photos.

The chair behind the oak desk was empty. May guessed the other meetings were taking place elsewhere on this floor.

"Look at all these trophies!" Owen exclaimed, walking over to see the silverware. "Football league, Champions League, and even an Olympic medal." He whistled. "This guy must be good. And these photos of all the teams he has managed—he has a history of success."

"Yes, he's clearly very good at what he does," May said. She guessed that would also make him a trusted figure. Had he abused that trust?

"That's him again," Owen said, pointing to a large framed photo of a man shaking hands with another premier league manager.

May ambled over and looked more closely, taking in his appearance and his confident, white-toothed smile. Everything about this man reeked of success.

"I wonder how long he'll be. I guess we sit and wait," May said.

"I guess so."

There was a table with a coffee machine, cream, cookies, pretzels, and even a decanter of brandy. Clearly, guests were encouraged to make themselves at home while waiting for the busy manager. She was sure potential sponsors would enjoy the spread, and feel as if they were going to get a great bang for their bucks. May thought this was all part of the show, giving the impression that Jessop was one of the state's most sought after businessmen and sports leaders.

But under all these trappings of success, was a monster hiding? Who was Jessop really, behind this moneyed facade?

She looked at the sofa, comfortable and squashy, wishing she felt more like relaxing on it, and not as if every moment counted.

She could see Owen didn't feel like sitting down either. Instead, May paced around the large space, taking a look out of the enormous window.

There was a magnificent view over suburbia that stretched as far as the sports fields of the training center down the road. So Jessop could sit here and watch his teams train, May thought. There was even a pair of binoculars on one of the tables. Right now, that gave her the creeps, because she didn't know if Jessop was a murderous predator. Were the binoculars there for looking at his teams, or had they been used to single out victims?

She wondered if there was any other viewpoint where he might have been able to look for prey. Craning her neck, she peered in the other direction.

May didn't see any other likely places where young women might congregate. But she saw something else.

She saw a dark-haired, well-groomed man in chinos and a black jacket.

He was heading down the fire escape on the corner of the building, looking stressed and furtive, his feet making faint clanging noises on the metal stairs.

May simply couldn't believe what she was seeing. Was she imagining things? Was this somebody else, and she was being overly paranoid? But then he turned to go down the next flight and she saw his face more clearly. She saw the strong jaw and the neatly groomed sideburns.

It was him.

"Owen!" May grabbed his arm. "Look there! That's Jessop, isn't it? It surely must be?"

"Where?"

"Come here and see for yourself!"

Owen rushed over to look.

"Yes, it's him. So what's he doing out there? Why is he going down the fire escape? He was supposed to be finishing a meeting and then joining us here!"

Very clearly he wasn't doing that.

"He's doing a runner," May concluded, utterly appalled by her own realization.

"He must have been expecting us, and he's running away because he knows we're going to question him about Emily's murder," Owen said.

This was a sign of guilt, so clear it astounded May.

"We need to get downstairs and stop him getting away. Quick, let's run." May didn't rate their chances if Jessop got behind the wheel of that powerful Mercedes.

May was already in motion as she spoke to Owen, bursting out of the plush office. They sprinted back to the elevator and slid in just as the doors were closing. The ride back down was fast, and when the doors opened, they stormed out.

The receptionist gave an astonished cry as May and Owen sped through the large lobby space. "What's going on?" she shouted, alarmed.

"Jessop! Jessop!" May shouted, heading full tilt for the parking lot. She hoped to goodness that once she got out, she would be in time to stop him.

There he was! Heading for the Mercedes, just a couple of yards from the car and moving fast.

"Jessop!" she yelled again.

He looked up and saw her. Horror filled his face. He dived for the car door.

May raced to cut him off. She was worried she was too late to stop him, but she knew that if she didn't, it might be difficult or impossible to catch him again.

But, with a gasp of triumph, Jessop swung himself into the seat. A moment later, the car roared to life.

CHAPTER TWENTY

"No!" May shouted, feeling stressed and frantic as Jessop revved the powerful Mercedes's engine. "Stop! Police!"

She'd yet to meet a guilty person who actually did stop when she said that. Jessop was no exception. He was clearly going to try and get away, and if he succeeded, she would have lost a strong suspect. It would delay the case. He might even be planning to flee and lie low, hiding from the police for as long as he could. Money always made things easier. Thoughts of private jets to countries without extradition treaties loomed in May's fevered imagination.

At the same time, her feet were pounding the concrete walkway toward the Merc, and her heart was racing.

She'd never expected him to do this! Had he made an exit plan that he was now actioning because the police had found out?

The thought of Kerry's face filled her mind. How she would look. Shocked and devastated by May's inadequacy if she allowed him to escape. Never mind that—the thought of her own disappointment in herself was impossible to imagine.

"Stop!" she screamed again.

She had only a nanosecond to decide what to do. He was already backing out of the bay. Following him in her car would leave her at a severe disadvantage and he'd leave her in his dust. And in any case, what would she do if the guards at the gate refused to raise the boom for her and prevented her from giving chase?

She had a dreadful feeling he was going to get away unless she did something. Anything.

The guards, she suddenly thought. The boom.

Already, the Mercedes was swinging around, and Owen had to leap out of the way of the veering hood or it would have hit him. Jessop gunned the motor, and the car shot forward.

But May had a new plan in mind.

She ran straight for the exit boom, her legs pistoning across the immaculate paving. This was the only way out. He'd have to take it.

With a smoking of tires, the Mercedes raced for the exit, heading for the boom, which the guards were already raising.

But May was fast enough to cross the short distance before Jessop got there. She leaped up, grabbed the boom, and with her full weight on the end of it, pulled it down so it was blocking the entrance.

Let him smash through it if he wanted, she thought, hanging on with grim determination. It was a solid boom, and it would wreck his car.

Jessop clearly reached the same conclusion.

Brakes shrieked. The car squealed to a stop, leaving black, smoking tracks behind it. The hood stopped an inch away from the boom.

In a moment, Owen was at the driver's door, pulling it open and yanking Jessop out. That was easy as he hadn't even had a chance to put on his seatbelt.

"What the hell do you think you're doing?" he yelled in panic at Owen. "Get your hands off me! This is private property, and you have no right to be here!"

"What do you think you're doing?" May said firmly. "You were supposed to be meeting with us. Not making a getaway down the fire escape."

He glowered at May, aghast and furious.

She looked him up and down, seeing his designer clothes, his well-groomed hair and sideburns, and his expensive shoes. Owen was still holding onto his arm firmly.

"I'm no criminal," he insisted.

"We're police officers!" May held up her ID for him to see. "You committed a felony by refusing to obey a direct request from an officer of the law."

Jessop was momentarily lost for words. His face twisted with rage, but after a moment he regained control.

"I don't know what you're talking about," he protested. "I never heard you say anything to me. I was told about a meeting elsewhere. I was late for it, and getting there as fast as I could. And you can let go of me. I'm innocent. I haven't done anything wrong."

"We're not letting go of you. We don't trust you," May insisted.

"Why don't you trust me?" He attempted a charming smile. "If you have any questions, you can ask me now. I have nothing to hide."

"You're going to have to come with us to police headquarters, Mr. Jessop," May said coldly. "And please prepare yourself to be fully cooperative. I'm sure we'll have plenty of time for questions when we get there."

*

Fifteen minutes later, May walked into the back office of the Chestnut Hill police department where they'd been working earlier.

As soon as Kerry saw her, she leaped up from the desk. She'd been hard at work, May saw. Three different laptops were open in a semi-circle surrounding her. On the other side of the room, Adams was busy taking screenshots of something official looking on a fourth laptop.

"May. Did you manage to get that footage?" Kerry asked. "I've been sending you a stream of information. I hope it's been useful?"

"I did better than that," May said. "We got the footage, showing Emily climbing into the car with him two weeks ago outside the sports center. And then we got Jessop."

"You brought him in?" Kerry looked impressed.

"Yes. He tried to run. It was totally surprising how fast he tried to avoid us. I mean, as soon as he heard we were police, he made a serious effort to get away. I wouldn't have thought that camera footage was so incriminating, but he clearly felt differently and knows more."

"Yes, he felt differently, but not only because of the camera footage," Kerry said, sounding smug.

"What do you mean?" May asked.

"Adams and I checked everything. Every last little detail. We are a very detail-oriented team, and we didn't want to overlook anything and have it come back to bite us. And one of the things Adams did, if you recall, was to get the bank statements from Mr. McGee, to check that his story about paying Shawna off was correct."

"And was it?" May asked.

She wondered where this was going. Had Kerry found something in those bank statements? She must have, to be looking so smug.

"Yes. Mr. McGee paid fifty thousand dollars into Shawna's bank account about twelve weeks ago."

"Fifty thousand dollars?" That was a sizeable payoff, May knew. She was surprised by the amount.

"But here's the thing. Two days before that payment was made, fifty thousand dollars was paid *into* Mr. McGee's account."

Kerry raised her eyebrows, looking mysterious.

"So you mean, someone loaned him or gave him the money?"

"Correct," Kerry said.

May put two and two together.

Glancing back at the interview room in shock, she spoke. "It wasn't—it couldn't have been—him?"

Kerry nodded. "Jessop loaned the McGees the money to pay Shawna off. It looks like he paid fifty thousand dollars from his bank account into Mr. McGee's bank account, shortly after she dropped the charges. She wanted compensation and she got it. From him."

"So Jessop has a very clear link to both women?" May said. "Emily climbed into his car on the day she disappeared, and three months earlier, he was responsible for Shawna's enormous payoff? No wonder he ran, if he figured we'd found that out."

"Yes. He paid money to silence one, and he rode away with the other in his car. I think his actions must be linked to his players and their reputations. But I'm sure he'll tell us more."

She tapped her fingers on the desk thoughtfully, glancing between her screens.

"There's a lot of money in the sport. Maybe having the threat of that lawsuit might compromise the sponsorships," May suggested.

"And maybe something similar played out with Emily. She was also Callum's ex. My feeling is he's trying to protect his team, and he realized both women were going to be a threat to its good name. So he set up the crime scene in a way that wouldn't make it seem it was him at all."

"Having interaction with both of the missing women is a very clear link," May said. She felt hugely impressed that Kerry had found this out.

"I think we've found our killer," Kerry said. "Let's go ask him and see if he can explain it away. We need to look for any evidence of a raft being made, and we need to lean on him heavily to tell us where Shawna is."

But as they stood up, May's phone rang.

"I'd better take it," she said. "It's Sheriff Jack."

As soon as she picked up, she heard how stressed her boss sounded.

"May, I have hard news. Shawna's body has been found."

"No!" May felt herself go sheet-white with shock. Kerry glanced at her in concern.

"It's been displayed the same way, on a homemade raft, and it's near the Chestnut Hill lumber yard."

"I'll get there right away."

May disconnected, feeling numb.

"The interview with Jessop will have to wait. We got him too late. Shawna's already dead." Her voice sounded small and shaky.

May felt tears prickling her eyes. She swiped at them with the back of her hand, overwhelmed by misery and regret. This was an absolute

92

tragedy. While they'd still been chasing down the convoluted trail leading to Jessop, he'd been committing a cold-blooded murder. Now, finally, she realized why he'd run from them so fast.

"We can't save her, but we can make sure we have all the evidence we need before we interrogate him. Let's get to the scene," Kerry said in a hard, level voice.

CHAPTER TWENTY ONE

May felt discouraged and filled with sadness as she headed out to the lake shore near the lumber yard. They were too late to prevent a tragedy. Another woman had died.

Would the scene offer any incriminating links to the suspect they had in custody?

May hoped so. It was all she could hope for now.

With her hands clenched on the wheel, and Owen sitting beside her in somber silence, she glanced into her mirror from time to time to make sure Kerry was following. She was, tailgating May in her usual impatient way.

There was the lumber yard ahead, and to the right of it, the road led down to the forested lake shore. She saw the familiar sight of the police cars parked there, the cars gleaming in the early afternoon sunshine.

She parked and climbed out, walking heavy-footed to the scene. Sheriff Jack hurried to meet them.

"Andy Baker is already on the scene and examining the body," he said. "I'm waiting for backup, and as soon as it arrives, I'm going to go and speak to Shawna's parents. I called them already to tell them this news. They asked me to call if we found her, but an in-person visit shows respect," he said.

"Agreed," Kerry said.

"You go down and ask Andy what you need to. We have to keep people away. We don't want this causing an uproar in the community. Not when we have a suspect in custody?"

He glanced at May.

Yet again, her stomach twisted. The pressure was now on. She hoped that she could find what she needed to link the arrogant Jessop to this scene. She knew she needed to observe as much as she could while they were here, because it would be very useful when questioning him. If they could get him to reveal a fact he shouldn't have known, that would be a big victory for them.

May trailed down the pathway to the lake shore. There, dressed in his gloves, mask, and protective gear, Andy Baker was at work.

"Afternoon, May," he said grimly. "Afternoon, Owen and Agent Kerry."

"What have you learned so far?" Kerry asked, stepping forward and clearly keen to take charge.

May knew how Kerry felt, because she was feeling the same. Burning with impatience, eager to charge Jessop with murder and put an end to this nightmare.

"As you can see, the modus operandi is identical," Andy said, indicating the raft.

It was exactly the same rough structure, with candles placed around the body. It was a still afternoon, and May saw to her shock a couple of the bigger ones were still burning low. That gave her a chill.

She stared down at this beautiful young woman, her life tragically cut short. Shawna had the face of an angel, with thick hair cascading down onto the wooden surface.

Her skin was ivory, a natural tan but no more. There was a delicate beauty mark close to her mouth.

She was gutted that they had come here too late. How could anyone be so cruel? Why would anyone want to kill another person like this? It gave May a sick feeling inside to think that both she and her sister were now here, staring down at a victim who was Lauren's age at the time she disappeared. She felt dizzy as past and present briefly collided. Then she dragged herself back to the current situation and forced her own ghosts aside.

She needed to assess this case, and the immediate impression was that he had sped up his timeline. Emily had been kept for two weeks before her death. But Shawna had only been kept overnight.

Why was that? May wondered. Was it just planning or logistics? Did the weather have anything to do with it? It had been rainy two weeks ago. Had he waited until the ground had dried, to cover his tracks better?

She noticed, to her surprise, that there was also one small flaw in this otherwise immaculate, funereal scene.

Shawna was wearing a top that was too small for her. May saw a button had snapped off, and a seam under the arm had ripped.

That brought back memories of the mismatched shoes. One of the shoes Emily had worn had also been too small.

What did it mean? Why was he placing one badly fitting item on each victim? Did it have significance, a message? Or was it just clever misdirection that meant nothing at all?

Andy cleared his throat, glancing up from his examination.

"The toxicology report for the first victim came back an hour ago. She was given a high dosage of sleeping pills, and then there is evidence she was smothered with something soft, as it left no marks."

May heard Kerry suck in a breath. She felt a chill down her spine too.

"And the pills? How would she have taken them?" May asked.

"They might have been dissolved in a very sweet drink. There was evidence of a chocolate drink in the stomach contents. Perhaps the girls were forced to take them, or encouraged or persuaded to. I'm not sure how that would have been done."

"How long ago did this victim die?" Kerry then asked.

"Probably she was murdered earlier this morning. It looks as if death occurred between five and seven hours ago."

"Five to seven hours," Kerry repeated thoughtfully, and May knew she was already assessing what Jessop's timeline would have had to be.

"Was she alive when she was placed on the raft?" May asked.

He shook his head. "I'd say unlikely."

"Any signs of vehicles, footprints?" Kerry then asked.

May looked around and cast her eyes over the calm lake. She looked at the trees and bushes on the other side, in the direction of the town. There were no obvious signs of car tracks, footsteps, or drag marks, and she wondered if there would be anything to find.

"I've had a walk around already." Jack spoke from behind her. Glancing back, May saw that another police car had pulled up and two new officers had taken over the job of guarding the scene from the small crowd that was gathering. "I didn't find anything. But the banks here are grassy and dry. There's not much opportunity to leave any signs."

"True," May said reluctantly.

She stared down at the victim in frustration, wishing that they had more they could use when they went back to Jessop.

"I'm going to go and visit Shawna's parents now. I hope your questioning is successful," Jack said. "I'm sure I don't need to tell you how urgent it is that we get results on this."

May nodded, feeling sick inside with tension. She could hear concerned voices ringing out from the growing crowd that was being kept well back by the police, but May could see several people were already on their phones.

Jack strode away, and Kerry stepped aside and began talking rapidly to Adams.

"I think you two gents should go straight out and conduct a search of Jessop's office premises, as well as his home and car. We need to look for any woodworking operations, any evidence of these rafts being constructed. We also need to see if he has tranquilizers or sleeping pills in his possession. These rafts could have been made in advance and left in prearranged places, or they could have been brought to the scene, but that would not have happened in that Mercedes, so let's check the other vehicles listed in his name."

Owen and Adams listened to Kerry intently, nodding as she spoke. May felt so impressed by Kerry's ability to take charge. She was such a natural leader, listing the salient points so concisely. It almost felt as if the case was already cut and dried, listening to her cool logic.

"We'll get straight onto that, and will call you as soon as we find anything," Adams said.

"Great." Kerry turned to May. "And now, I guess the two of us need to get back to the police department as quickly as we can and interview Jessop. Now that we have more information on the scene, we can try to trip him up. Or trap him," Kerry suggested, with a predatory gleam in her eye that told May she was committed to this takedown.

CHAPTER TWENTY TWO

"You need to explain yourself, Mr. Jessop, because we have a solid ton of evidence against you here."

May watched admiringly, standing inside the interview room's doorway as Kerry started out with the interrogation. She was going in hardcore, unsmiling, her perfect jaw jutting out as she stared him down, her laser-like blue eyes seeming to drill holes into him. With Kerry on force level ten, the small room felt positively claustrophobic, May thought.

Mr. Jessop was seated in a chair on the opposite side of the desk. He was already sweating noticeably.

"I've told you, I don't know anything about this crime at all," Jessop insisted, his voice shaking slightly.

May kept her expression devoid of emotion, but she was beside herself with tension. She was desperate for Jessop to slip up, to give himself away.

"Emily was seen getting into your car just before she disappeared. And you paid Shawna off via the McGees. What's the deal there?" Kerry threatened.

"Look, I can explain."

"Well, explain then."

"You see, the bottom line, the main concern, is this."

"Is what?"

"I really care for my players."

May stared at him cynically as he elaborated on this.

"I really care for my players. I just want to help them if I can. I'm told that if you can just focus the mind, and bring a certain perspective to the challenges you are facing, you can make the world seem a better place."

"Interesting choice of words," Kerry said, focusing ever more intently on him.

"You mean, how I care for my players?"

"I mean, bringing a certain perspective to the challenges you face."

Jessop paled.

"I've proven that in the past, have I not? I've placed so much time and care into developing their skills and their confidence. I do everything I can to ensure they can reach their full potential. They are an investment financially, sure, I admit that. Sponsors pay for players, for personalities. But also, I value them as people."

"And that's why you felt you had to kill two women?" Kerry asked.

"I did not kill anybody," Jessop insisted, his eyes darting from side to side.

May was proud of Kerry's tenacity, and she forced herself to remain still and silent. But she needed Jessop to confess, to give himself away; they were out of options at this point.

"I care about my players. I care about their welfare. I'm deeply invested in their development. I genuinely am committed to the success of this team. This town is my home. I'm a local boy. I care about the community."

"We're not talking about your team. This is about two murders. Why did Emily get into your car?" Kerry pressed him.

"I—I needed to speak to her."

May felt a flare of excitement that he was starting to explain. She wondered where this would lead.

"Why? She's not on your football team."

Jessop let out a frustrated sigh. "Look, I know this will be difficult for you to understand."

"Try me," Kerry challenged.

"I've been trying to explain. That we need to look after these players personally. Now Callum. Let's talk about Callum. One of our most talented quarterbacks. In fact, to be honest, our only decent quarterback. There's nobody else who makes the grade. For some reason they are in very short supply here."

"Your point being?"

"He is a brilliant player. But if he has personal problems, his game goes out the window. He loses focus completely, he makes rookie errors. It's like watching someone who's never played football before."

"So what are you saying?"

"I'm saying that as the team manager, it was my responsibility to make sure that Callum was happy. That he was stable and not emotionally unbalanced. And when he had girlfriend issues, he became emotionally unbalanced."

"Right. So you killed the women to make sure he was on an even keel?" Kerry asked briskly. "Thanks for that information."

"No, no!" Jessop wrung his hands together. "I killed nobody! But I counseled the girls. I will admit, I told Emily that she should give up on the idea of getting back together with him. That was why we went for that drive. I wanted to explain to her what a bad idea it would be. To give her an adult perspective on how unstable it would inevitably be."

"Where did you drive?" Kerry asked.

"To the park. I think it's called Braeside Park. Anyway, I wanted her to understand that if she went back to Callum, it would all end badly. But she didn't just accept what I said. She discussed it with me. I mean, we had a real heart to heart. We had ice creams, if I remember. Unfortunately, I paid cash for them, and I have no idea who the vendor was. Eventually she saw it my way. Then I dropped her off at home. I have no idea where she went afterward. But anyway, the fact is, I'm the one who has to manage the team, right? I have to maintain the team ethos, the team unity."

"So what happened with Shawna?"

"Now that was a difficult situation. There was fault on both sides, absolutely. But Callum was emotionally distraught, simply as a result of the rollercoaster ride he was on. Eventually we saw light at the end of the tunnel. She was happy with his apology and the photos being deleted, but she needed something more concrete, a financial commitment that Callum stood by his words. So since Callum's father was not currently in a situation to provide that, and he didn't want his ex-wife to know anything about it in case she started demanding more alimony, I helped out on a confidential basis."

"So you're saying you paid her to make her go away. That is what you are saying?" Kerry clarified.

He spread his hands, a vestige of an innocent smile trembling on his face.

"Well, sure. I guess that's what I'm saying."

May felt momentarily conflicted. Jessop was admitting to his reasons very openly. Would he be doing that if he had murdered the young women? Was he, in fact, being truthful?

Kerry clearly didn't think they had the whole truth yet. She raised her eyebrows challengingly, and Jessop continued.

"I also did it out of the goodness of my own heart. I could see she was in a difficult situation, that she needed some comfort, and I wanted to help her out. I think all of us saw that the relationship was over. And it was better for the team that she was gone. I didn't want the distraction."

"I see," Kerry said.

"It's all about the big picture strategy. For my team, that is. We are like a family. We all pull together for the greater good. I don't interfere where I don't have to, you see. I can tell you now, honestly, those were the only two problematic relationships Callum had. It's just a very unlucky coincidence that both of these women have been involved in—in this other business, with whoever is doing this."

Kerry gave a tiny shake of her head. May could see that Kerry was totally unimpressed with this story. That she thought Jessop was a liar and a money-hungry user who had no conscience whatsoever.

The problem was that May didn't entirely share her views. May thought that deep down, Jessop might be telling the truth. Weird though they were, she could see that this was how things in a small town worked. You wanted something, you used the personal touch to get it.

"Well, we'll leave you here for a while," Kerry said, checking her phone. "I see my partner has given me a progress report on the search he's doing. We need to get up to speed on that. I'm sure he has interesting information to share with us."

She stared intensely at Jessop, who went pale. Clearly, he was worried about the search.

He looked a lot like a deer trapped in headlights. He knew he was in deep trouble and he was unable to figure out a way out of this mess.

May couldn't wait to hear the details, and if Adams had given some actual information in that quick text update. Hopefully if he had, it would provide a stronger framework to take this case forward.

"We'll leave you here to think things through," Kerry said. "But we'll be back for a proper chat later. I'm sure by then, you'll be ready to tell us more."

She stood up and stalked out, with May behind her.

CHAPTER TWENTY THREE

Owen walked into Jessop's house, following Adams, who was making sure to take the lead in the important job of searching the suspect's home premises. Owen was easygoing enough not to mind. He just hoped there was something to be found, because if they could find evidence that firmly linked Jessop to these crimes, then this traumatizing case would be wrapped up.

He didn't mind if Adams found it first. As long as it was found.

As someone who had made a career move relatively late in life, joining the police at the age of twenty-nine, he was used to being the junior and Adams was undoubtedly the senior.

But Owen resolved to search as thoroughly as he could. And not just for Adams. He didn't want to let May down.

Adams pushed open the door, after unlocking it with the key that Jessop had signed over to them before he'd been taken into the interview room.

"Fancy house," he commented.

Owen agreed. "Yeah, he is definitely not struggling for money."

The two-story home was located in a magnificent hilltop stand in a secure gated estate about two miles from Jessop's office.

The architectural style was rather plain and modern, but the setting and position were stunning. He had a fantastic view, which was probably why he'd chosen this place to live.

Inside, Owen saw the furniture was ostentatious and looked brand new. It looked like it had been carefully chosen to make a statement, rather than to be comfortable. The chandeliers were so gaudy, Owen had to blink in the light.

In the living room, there were pictures of Jessop with various famous people, including top sports people. There were awards, footballs, and trophies in cabinets along the walls.

"I'm going to search upstairs, with particular focus on unearthing any sedatives, sleeping tablets, or other tranquilizing drugs," Adams uttered, chin jutted.

"Okay," Owen said.

"You search the garages, all four of them, and both the outbuildings. With particular focus on any woodworking tools. I've

102

detailed the types of nails and wood used in the first raft. The specs are here with me. Now they're with you."

With a flourish, Adams sent the details to Owen's iPad.

"Let's touch base in half an hour and see what progress we've made," Adams announced, as if he was a sergeant major giving orders to an army of one.

"Absolutely," Owen agreed enthusiastically. There was no harm in Adams being self-important. As long as evidence was found.

This case was so big, so worrying, so downright weird. It was consuming all their focus, Owen knew. He couldn't wait for it to be solved, to know that the killer who was committing these sadistic crimes, taking young lives and devastating families, was firmly behind bars.

Then he could get back to the usual worries of his life, such as his workload, and the upcoming salary reviews in July, and of course, whether he would ever be able to ask May on a real date.

Not a sort-of going for drinks date, but a proper date, with dinner and wine, at a fancy restaurant, and maybe dancing afterward. He had a shortlist of two places that he couldn't wait to book.

But he had to wait, because life was complicated and dating work colleagues was tricky. Especially in the police, and especially since he was so shy about it, and it meant so much to him, that he kept messing it up. And he wasn't sure if May really wanted to, or if it would even be the right decision.

Putting these thoughts aside, Owen put on his gloves and foot covers and headed outside to the side door that led into the quadruple garages.

He began with the first garage, which was occupied by a massive SUV, an Audi A8. With the crime in mind, Owen noted that this vehicle had a spacious trunk and could easily have transported a raft, plus victim. The darkly tinted windows would certainly have been an advantage.

He opened the trunk and checked it carefully. He ran his gloved hands along the interior, but no piece of wood or nails were in evidence.

Next, he checked the second and third garages. The second one was home to an Aston Martin, and the third one contained a low-slung vintage Lotus. Both were immaculately clean. The final garage was empty and locked, presumably the home of the Mercedes.

With a frown, he went back outside and headed over to the outbuildings.

In the first building, he found nothing of interest. It was a storage shed, with old boxes and a lot of gym and sporting equipment piled up.

In the second building, he found more useful evidence. Opening the door, he felt a flare of excitement as he stared into the neat, but dusty space.

The spacious room was clearly used as a workshop. It smelled of sawdust and oils. On the floor, he could see discarded pieces of wood and nails. There were several power tools and saws on brackets on the wall, and there were at least twenty boxes of nails and screws and hinges and fittings, all of different sizes.

Owen guessed that the nails used in making the raft, which were a common size, would definitely be in one of the boxes.

Owen photographed the evidence carefully and double-checked the specs of the nails, working methodically, knowing that the photos he took now and the records he noted down might be used in a court of law to prove Jessop's guilt. Responsibility weighed heavy on him as he worked through the room.

This was what fighting crime was all about, and why he found it fascinating. It was partly action, danger, controlling someone who was violent and chasing down a suspect. But it was also this collection of evidence, which was so important and where the small details could make a huge difference.

Finally, Owen felt he'd done a thorough job that May would be proud of. Checking the time, he saw it was almost time to meet up with Adams. He hoped that he'd also had a successful search.

Owen headed back to the front of the house and saw Adams coming downstairs. He, too, wore gloves and foot covers, as well as a satisfied expression.

"There were several packets of sleeping tablets and barbiturates in the master bathroom. Definitely strong enough to be effective in sedating the victims. The other interesting thing I found is that there's a soundproof movie room in the basement."

"Seriously?" Owen asked.

"Yes. It's soundproof with a lockable door. So potentially, he could have held the victims in there without anyone hearing."

"That's interesting," Owen agreed. He'd been wondering how Emily had been held captive for so long without managing to alert anyone. He'd been imagining a remote location. But a soundproofed room would also work.

"I found a well-equipped workshop, with evidence of woodworking and the right type of nails," he said.

"Excellent!" Adams praised. "Now, let's go back to the offices and have a look in his personal vehicle, the Merc. He seems to use that for his everyday work, so there might well be something useful inside."

They climbed into the unmarked and Adams started it up, setting off on the short drive back to Jessop's offices.

Owen felt energized by how well they were doing. With any luck, this evidence would provide what was needed to prove the case.

They pulled into the offices, where the Mercedes was parked in the bay closest to the boom. One of the guards had moved it away from the boom and then Owen had taken the keys. Now, he took them out of his pocket and climbed out of the unmarked's passenger seat.

He pressed the remote to unlock the doors and they snapped open.

Owen opened the trunk and stared inside.

His eyes widened in surprise.

"This is interesting. Very interesting," he said to Adams.

Adams stared down and Owen heard him draw in a shocked breath.

"Now, that is more than interesting. We need to take this car to the police department," he decided. "This might just be the last piece of evidence we need. I want Kerry to see it, and confront Jessop with it, while they're still questioning him."

CHAPTER TWENTY FOUR

Stepping outside the interview room, May saw Adams and Owen walking briskly into the department. She hoped their arrival meant they had found something that would add serious proof to this case. Adams looked excited. Owen looked resolute.

She knew that the evidence showed Jessop had a strong motive for silencing both girls. They were causing stress to one of his star players, who was needed to fill a key position on the field, and whose performance was suffering.

May had seen for herself how much money was in this sport at top level. It was no surprise that the desire to succeed might cause a team manager to go as far as murder.

But where May was having doubts was believing that Jessop would go about it that way. He didn't seem like the kind of person who would create such an elaborate scenario. The whole affair seemed too complex, too theatrical, too contrived.

Why would he have done this? It seemed to have been done by someone for whom this meant something. What had been created in this raft scenario was somehow important to the killer. It was significant to him. In his damaged mind, setting out the victims on the raft was completing—something—that he felt needed to be complete.

That was what she concluded, from what she had seen of the crimes so far. Jessop was a straightforward businessman. Practical, quick, impatient.

If he'd committed murder, May thought he would have done it differently.

For now, May knew she was just going by her instincts. And her instincts were telling her to be careful about jumping to conclusions. Her instincts were telling her the killer's mind worked differently.

Too many things didn't quite fit with their theory and so May was still worried that they were building a case around a man who might be innocent. Given that the case was so high profile, with the media following it closely, any mistake would be front-page news.

She could imagine it now: "Police accuse team manager of murder, but fail to prove it."

May hoped that whatever Owen and Adams had uncovered would be the game-changer they needed.

"We have evidence of woodworking in an outbuilding at his home, with supplies of the same nails used. We found strong sedatives and sleeping tablets in his bathroom," Adams announced proudly.

May gasped. But there was more, it seemed.

"And we brought in his car," Adams said. "There's something in it you need to see, now."

May exchanged an excited glance with Kerry. Together, they rushed outside.

Owen put on his gloves again before opening the car's trunk.

May stared down, drawing in a breath.

There were several pairs of shoes in the trunk. The shoe shape and color were familiar.

They were exactly the same type of white shoe that Emily Hobbs had been wearing when her body was laid out on the raft. These shoes were identical to the mismatched shoe that had been forced onto her right foot.

These shoes were bigger, though, May noted. And they were all pairs. There were no single shoes among them.

"Those are lacrosse cleats," Adams said. "I used to play."

"They are?" Kerry asked in surprise, as if astounded to learn that her partner possessed this talent.

"Yes. But these are men's shoes. I think the one on the victim's foot was a ladies' shoe, from the photographs. Still, this could be your proof," Adams told her.

"Yes, it could," Kerry said.

May stared down at the shoes, feeling a flare of excitement and hope. Perhaps her misgivings had been wrong.

"He's a team manager. Surely there is a reasonable explanation for why he has these shoes in his car?" Owen asked.

Kerry was ready with some possible theories.

"The killer has the shoes available. In a moment of madness, he sees the opportunity to add to the scene of a murder. Perhaps he did it because he wanted to personally feel satisfaction at the link to playing sports."

"That's a good theory," Adams said.

"Maybe he liked to torture her. He enjoyed seeing her in pain and he forced her to wear that small shoe to make her uncomfortable," Kerry then said.

Adams nodded knowingly.

"Like the Hobart case," he said to Kerry.

"Exactly. The Hobart case is the perfect example. He was also a successful businessman, quite similar to Jessop. And he had a deeply sadistic side that was well hidden."

"Yes," Adams said.

"How about the shirt?" May asked. "Shawna was found with a too-small shirt."

Kerry nodded. "That is a standard sport shirt. Can be used for any sport, including lacrosse. So the link is still there. Sports. That's why he killed. To protect his team."

"Or, the sadism link is there, too. Force the victim to wear small clothing to make her uncomfortable," Adams said.

"We've also got the evidence of woodworking in his home, and that he had sleeping pills in his possession. The circumstantial evidence is now very strong," Kerry stated. "I think we need to go in for another round of questioning with Jessop."

"Agreed. Let's confront him with all this evidence. And go at him hard, he needs to crack now," Adams said.

"I think you should come in with me, Adams," Kerry said to him. "Let's us two go and do that approach we used with Hobart. It worked then, and I am sure it will work again."

"I think that's the right approach." Adams gave her a confident grin.

Together, the two of them turned and strode back into the police department.

May couldn't help but feel totally sidelined. She looked down, not wanting Owen to see how ashamed she felt. Kerry and Adams were such a strong team. May had tried so hard to be of value to this case, but what had she done? Nothing! At least Owen had uncovered useful information. May's sole contribution to the success of this investigation had been breathing some of the air in the interview room, and frowning sternly at Jessop when Kerry asked a question.

She racked her brain for something constructive she could do now that would help to move the case forward while the two agents were doing their high-pressure questioning.

As she paced up and down outside the police department, a car pulled up and a harassed-looking woman scrambled out.

"Good afternoon," she said breathlessly.

May could see she had been crying. She looked in her early forties, and also vaguely familiar. May thought she'd seen her around town before.

"Good afternoon, ma'am. How can we help?" she asked politely, hurrying over to the citizen in need.

"My daughter's missing!" the woman said.

May's eyes widened.

"Missing? Since when?" A chill went through her.

"She was sent home from school at eleven thirty. She never arrived home. She was supposed to call me and say she was being dismissed early due to a bullying incident. And now, her younger sister just got home and told me all of this. Chanel is nowhere. Her phone's turned off. And I'm convinced this killer has taken her. Please, please, help me find my daughter!"

The woman burst into tears.

CHAPTER TWENTY FIVE

"It's okay, ma'am. You need to stay calm," May said, escorting the woman into the police department. But she didn't feel calm inside at all. Stress bubbled up inside her at the thought another girl was missing.

She led the woman to the tidy front desk and handed her a Kleenex.

"I'm so sorry. I'm so sorry I'm crying in front of you," the woman said, dabbing at her eyes.

"It's okay. It's normal to feel upset," May said. "You must be very stressed now. But I please need you to stay calm and try to recall as many facts as you can."

"I—I will," the woman whispered.

"I'm Deputy Moore. What's your name?"

"Shayla South."

"I appreciate you coming in to speak to us. Please take a seat and we'll get someone to get you a cup of coffee," May said. She turned to Owen, who nodded and headed for the small kitchenette at the back of the police department.

"Thank you," the woman said gratefully, sinking down into one of the chairs.

"Mrs. South, I'm going to bring you a clipboard. You will need to make a statement giving your full name, address, and a detailed description of the circumstances behind your daughter's disappearance. The name of the school, the route she would have taken home. All these can help us."

"It's Chestnut Hill High," Mrs. South blurted out, accepting the pen and clipboard from May, and May felt another pang of panic inside her. She glanced at Owen, who was returning with the coffee, seeing her emotions reflected in his eyes.

Chestnut Hill High was the school the killer was targeting.

"How old is your daughter?" she asked.

"She's eighteen."

May's lips tightened. Again, this was the age the killer was choosing. She felt anxiety flare inside her as the woman carefully completed the statement, her hand shaking.

Meanwhile, May's mind was racing.

110

She was thinking about the timeline. If this daughter had left school at eleven thirty a.m. there was no way Jessop could have taken her. Because at that time, without a doubt, he had been inside those expensive offices and nowhere else.

She'd felt there were some inconsistencies that made it unlikely he was the killer, and now this incident was proving it.

That made May feel a heightened sense of panic, because where else was there to look? They'd been through this case in so much detail. Jessop was a strong suspect, linked to both the girls with compelling evidence. The video, the payment.

If they had to start again, she felt sick with fear that they might just come up blank.

On the positive side, Chanel had disappeared recently. She'd been gone only a few hours. Surely that meant they had time? Although what use was time, when they had no idea where to look?

"Can you please give me the names of all your daughter's friends that you know of?" May said, glad her voice sounded relatively calm. She wasn't sure what to do. This was another lead, another girl who could be in danger. And she had no idea where to start looking.

"You think she might have gone to one of them?" Mrs. South said, looking up at her with what May now saw was forlorn hope.

She didn't want to give her unfounded hope.

"We need to rule out every possibility. We must explore every avenue that she could have taken," she said.

"Oh, okay. I don't think she would have done so because all her friends were at school. But I'll give you the numbers."

She wrote frantically on the page.

"Breena Michaels?" May read.

"Yes, that's her best friend."

"Have you called her yet?" May asked.

Mrs. South nodded. "Yes, I've called her. She's been at school. She hasn't seen Chanel."

"And the others?"

"Logan Laroche and Marissa Salem. Marissa was with Breena. I haven't called Logan yet. I thought I'd rather come here first. In any case, Logan lives far out of town."

"Okay. I'll get someone to call Logan," May said.

May looked down at her address and then glanced over at the set of town maps that were mounted on the wall. There were ten maps there, representing the ten biggest lakeside towns. Mounting those maps had been May's idea, and one of the first projects she'd done as the new deputy. They had proven to be very useful, because people could easily point out where crimes had occurred. Chestnut Hill's map had a pale orange background. Estimating the distance between the school and the home, May guessed it was about four or five miles. It was a long way to walk, especially on such a hot day.

It made it even more likely that the killer might have opportunistically offered her a ride, and that this girl would have accepted.

Mrs. South passed the completed paperwork over the counter. Then she handed May a picture of Chanel. Like the others, May noticed this young woman was very pretty. She had green eyes and shiny, shoulder-length brown hair. She could see the resemblance to her mother.

She glanced at Owen, and her heart nearly broke at the bleak expression on his face. They were looking at another girl who had a chance of being the next victim.

"We are prioritizing this case," she told the distraught woman. "We will do everything in our power to find your daughter."

"She doesn't bully. My daughter is not a bully," Mrs. South insisted.

"You think she was sent home unfairly?"

"Yes. She's told me before now who the bullies in that school are. They often get sent home and get demerit points. My Chanel is not like that. But I'm sure she was standing up to them, either for herself or for Briony, her younger sister. I'm sure that is what happened. Briony's been bullied before now. That school has a big problem. It has for years. I've been thinking of pulling my daughters from it. Now I wish I had. If I'd done that, this would never have happened!"

"I understand, Mrs. South," Owen said.

May let the woman talk. She needed to talk. And it was important to listen, May knew. Perhaps something she said might end up being helpful to the case. There were also questions she needed to confirm from her side.

"Was there anything else going on in your daughter's life?" May asked, knowing the question could be important. "Any problems, any issues with boyfriends, any experiments with drugs or alcohol? Anything that was out of the ordinary recently that you noticed?"

"No. Honestly, no. I'm not just saying that. She was a good girl. She didn't get into that sort of trouble. She has a boyfriend that she writes to. They have an online relationship. He lives in New York."

"Thank you," May said gently.

"What do I do now?" Mrs. South asked, weeping.

"I need you to please stay calm. Stay home, make sure that your other daughter is safe and has her family with her. Contact me if you hear anything, or if you think of any other leads you would like us to follow up."

"I'll do that."

"If you hear from Chanel, call me immediately. The phone numbers I am giving you are for me and my partner who is working this case."

"Thank you."

"You're welcome to sit here for a while until you feel calm enough to drive home. Or if you like, my partner will give you a ride home."

But Mrs. South did look calmer now. She finished her coffee and stood up.

"I'll be okay to drive," she said. "I'll head home now and stay with Briony."

"We'll be in touch," May said gently, hoping that when they did get in touch, it would be with good news. But that was no certainty, and in fact might not even be a possibility.

This changed the whole landscape of the investigation. It was potentially a new disaster. She knew she had to go and tell Kerry immediately.

Together, she hoped, they could come up with a new plan of action, a new angle, to hunt this killer down.

CHAPTER TWENTY SIX

"This is terrible," Owen whispered to May as soon as Mrs. South had left, and she nodded, agreeing with him. It was more than terrible. It was a potential disaster. There was another victim taken, May was sure of it. The parameters were too similar to be ignored. Three victims might die at this killer's hands.

The man in custody could not have taken Chanel, and May was at a loss to know who else could have.

"We need to go and tell Kerry urgently," May said.

Owen made a face. "I guess we do," he said.

May could see he also didn't want to interrupt her, derail her questioning, and present her with this new bombshell.

And there was always the slim chance that this young woman had genuinely gone off to a friend's house after being kicked out of school for the day. They had no proof yet that she was the killer's third victim.

Only a strong feeling.

"Shall we go and watch from the observation room?" May decided. "That way, we can step in at the right moment?"

She also harbored a hope that perhaps Jessop would confess to the crimes. That would also mean that hopefully Chanel South was hiding away from the trouble she thought would descend at home, rather than being held by the killer and in terrible danger.

They hurried to the observation room. May couldn't help the frantic thoughts from whirling round and round in her brain.

Another girl was missing. That meant that they were running out of time. And that scared her. Very, very much.

She had to try to keep calm, keep focused.

It was only when they were in the observation room that May realized this was the first time she and Owen had been alone together in such a small space in a long time.

In the cubbyhole-sized room, they were squashed together, shoulder to shoulder. May caught the faint scent of Owen's deodorant, which to her smelled like sandalwood. She could smell a hint of mint from his shampoo. And she could feel his arm, warm and firm against hers as they peered through the window.

Inside, Kerry was on her feet, screaming at Jessop.

"And you're going to sit there and tell me that you don't know anything about these girls?" she was saying, her face flushed with anger. "That's a lie, Mr. Jessop. A bare-faced lie!"

"It contradicts what you said earlier!" Adams added. He was clearly being the calm voice of reason, while Kerry was playing the role of the aggressor to get him to break.

"I'm not saying that," Jessop said in quavering tones.

"You're not saying you did it, but you're not saying you didn't. What do you think you're doing now? Your version is all over the place. Are you unable to coordinate your lies anymore?" Kerry demanded.

"I'm telling you the truth," Jessop said, his voice shaking.

"You did it!" she shouted. "I know you did. Those girls needed to be removed because of the interests of your team. You removed them, and you did it permanently! It's obvious. A jury won't have any trouble accepting this version based on the compelling evidence. So now, we're talking about pleas."

"If you plead guilty, you'll have an easier time of it, every step of the way," Adams said, his voice persuasive. "Perhaps there are other factors that you're not telling us. Medication you were on at the time, anyone who helped you? Telling the truth will be the best decision, that I promise. Juries hate killers who lie."

"But I didn't do it," Jessop said. "I had nothing to do with it. It wasn't me."

"You had everything to do with it. Every single thing. There's no way around this. Admit what you did and you might get off slightly better," Kerry said.

"I'll get you everything you need to make it work," Adams promised. "I'll get you the best lawyer in the business. The evidence is there, you can't lie and say that it isn't."

"I—I really didn't do it. I mean, I don't remember doing it," Jessop stammered.

"What do you mean by that last statement?" Adams said. "Are you saying you have had memory blanks in the past?" Now he sounded calm and caring.

"I—I need to go to the bathroom," Jessop gasped.

Kerry and Adams exchanged a glance.

"Take him," Kerry snapped out.

Adams practically lifted Jessop to his feet. He looked worn out, terrified, and confused, as if their high pressure questioning was making him wonder if he had committed these crimes in a hallucinogenic moment.

"We'd better go now," May whispered.

She and Owen bundled out of the observation room and rushed around to the interview room door.

There, Kerry was standing, looking satisfied, as Adams hustled Jessop down the corridor.

"Did you hear some of that?" she asked, seeing them approach. "It's going really well. We're getting somewhere. We're starting to break down his defenses and get close to the truth."

May took a deep breath. "There's been a complication," she said. She knew this was not the right moment for this news. It wouldn't go down well.

Kerry's brow wrinkled slightly.

"What do you mean by that?"

"I mean that another girl is missing. Chanel South. Her mother's just come in and reported it."

Kerry's eyes widened. "When did she go missing?"

May felt panic surge inside her again. "Just now. I mean, at half past eleven. Somewhere around that time. She was sent home from school after a fight. From Chestnut Hill High."

May felt painfully conscious that she was babbling out her story, not presenting it coherently. Under Kerry's critical gaze, with time so tight, she was fumbling her elevator pitch.

"You're not making sense. So this girl disappeared today, at half past eleven? After being sent home? Did she not arrive home?"

May took a deep breath.

"She's not been seen since she left school," she said. "She apparently didn't go home. Her mother only found out now, when her younger sister arrived. Her phone is off. She's called a couple of her friends and she's not there."

"She was sent home from school in trouble. And if they allowed her to walk, any right-thinking person would go and spend time somewhere else," Kerry said. "Who would go home knowing you were going to be in trouble? What kind of school allows such a policy?" she asked herself in mystified tones.

"She's a good girl, cleaner than clean. Her mother didn't think she would just run away."

Kerry sighed.

"She might not have run away, but be hiding out. Laying low. That's most likely what she's doing."

"But she could be in danger!"

"So you're saying she's in danger, based on what? A feeling? A suspicion? A hunch? You're basing all of this on nothing?"

"Not nothing," May said, trying to keep her cool. "I have a very strong feeling that something terrible has happened. I feel that she's the killer's next victim."

How she wished she was presenting this argument more persuasively. But she wasn't, and Kerry did not seem convinced.

"We are about to break Jessop. I'm sure of it. He's showing all the signs," she said firmly. "There's no way I'm derailing this interrogation now. It's been what, three or four hours since Chanel was sent home? That's far too soon to panic, especially since the strong suspect in custody is about to confess."

May felt herself blush. She was getting nowhere with Kerry.

"We have no alternatives," her sister said. "We have to pursue this interrogation and take it all the way to the wire. We have to break this guy. I can't stop now. If I do, we might never get answers from him, and we need answers. We need details."

"So what do we do about Chanel?"

Kerry shook her head. "Look, May, you're the local police. Do I have to tell you what to do?" she said impatiently. "Treat it the same as you would any missing person case. Follow leads, question people along the route she took, call her friends. In fact, maybe go visit her friends. They might be protecting her. That's policing 101. You should already know how to do it." She gave May a superior smile, and May blushed even deeper. She was being told off, and told how to do her job, and all in front of Owen, which made it even worse.

"If we don't break him, we'll certainly get to Chanel. But for now, you sort that out. I have a suspect to interrogate. Please, no more interruptions, no matter what. We're reaching a critical stage now," Kerry said, turning her head in the direction of the returning footsteps.

With a despairing sigh, May trailed away, heading for the back office.

The pain and worry in the mother's eyes felt etched in her mind. She knew this was linked. She felt it. But she hadn't been able to persuade her sister how serious she thought this was.

She slumped down at the desk. Owen sat down opposite her.

"May, I believe you. I think you're right," he said earnestly.

She shook her head, unwilling to even look at him.

"Kerry won't take it seriously. And she's the FBI agent. Maybe we're wrong. If we try to push it, we might end up damaging the case."

Owen shook his head stubbornly. "You're the best investigator I know. You've never damaged a case. You always have the best personal insight into a situation, and can read people better than anyone else. I believe in you, May."

She stared at him, surprised by the emotion in his words, feeling a surge of gratitude for his unwavering support. In fact, she found herself blushing again. There was something about the tone of his voice that reinforced to her this was not just professional praise. He was sharing his own personal feelings for her, and that made her feel strangely short of breath.

"What if there's another explanation for this, another reason behind it, that we haven't thought of yet?" he continued.

"Do you really think there is?" May asked. She realized how much she trusted his insight, too. If he instinctively felt there was more still to explore, then May was going to take that seriously.

"There might be," Owen insisted. "We're the locals. We have local knowledge, May. What aren't we seeing? What have we missed, in all the excitement with the FBI getting involved?"

May raised her head and stared into Owen's brown eyes. He looked like he meant what he said. He wasn't just saying it to comfort her. And his argument was sound. They did have local knowledge, and hadn't used it enough so far.

"Maybe we have missed something," she said. "Let's get the file and have one more look."

CHAPTER TWENTY SEVEN

Sitting in the back office, feeling as if the pressure was bearing down on her like an actual weight, May pulled together everything they had on the case so far. It was disturbingly little. The evidence was scanty. From a missing person case, to having two murder victims; things had escalated in the space of a day.

Now a third had been taken. She was sure of it. The killer was gaining confidence. Perhaps becoming reckless. Or having started, he was now on an unstoppable arc that would only end with his arrest or death. Until then, the whole community might remain in danger.

"Does Chanel South have any connection with Callum? Any connection with any football player?" Owen asked.

That was a good idea, May thought. Involvement with Jessop needed to be ruled out. But she shook her head. "If there's one, it's so weak that not even her mother knew about it. She's in a long-distance relationship. And Jessop did mention that Shawna and Emily had been the only two problematic relationships for Callum."

"So either it's not connected, and she's gone for a different reason, or it is connected. With the other disappearances, I mean," Owen said. "And if it is connected, then it means it's someone else. Which is what I feel we've both suspected for a while."

"Yes. It was the theatrics of the scene that made me feel there was more to it."

"Exactly." Owen nodded intently. "It was telling a story. I thought to myself, when I saw that, it was someone wanting us to see something. Not just see it, but perceive it his way."

"If Jessop was a murderer—which I don't think he is—I feel he would have done things differently."

"Exactly. And he didn't need to kill anyone. With pockets as deep as his, he could just pay people off. That's much more effective, really. Money talks. And if it's done in the right way, you don't go to jail," Owen said thoughtfully.

May glanced at him, feeling startled.

"Sorry," Owen said. "It's my accounting background, before joining the police. You know, my past job was pretty routine most of the time, but occasionally it was fascinating. We did forensic investigations into a couple of clients on behalf of people. We came across that once or twice," Owen explained.

"I see," May said.

What Owen had said about the past was making her think. There was something nagging at her mind. A faint memory. No more than a ghost of a thought.

The past. What did it mean?

"There's something I want to remember but I can't, and I think it's important. I'm sure of it. Something that happened a while ago, but I can't figure out what it is," she said, frustrated.

She knew she needed to remember, but she couldn't. At this moment of high pressure, the memory was elusive.

May began to worry it would escape her forever, or at least for long enough to be useless to her in figuring out this case.

"You're trying too hard," said Owen. "Think about something else and maybe it will come to you."

"Something else? At this time?" May sighed. She couldn't get her mind off the case. "Let's go back and look at old news articles. Maybe that will help with the memories."

"Yes, that's a good idea." Looking thoughtful, Owen turned to his laptop. Then he turned back again. "What should we search for?"

"I don't know. We need to identify some parameters that will connect with what's happening now."

"Callum? The McGees? Perhaps there's something on them, going back?"

"Let's take a look. That's a good starting point."

Feeling hopeful, May moved to the computer. She typed in Mr. McGee's name and searched. She added the key words crime, murder, arrest. Then she tried the same with Mrs. McGee and Callum.

"Nothing is coming up," she said. She drummed her fingers on the desk in annoyance.

"So then we need to search for something different. Widen the parameters," Owen suggested.

"The families of the victims?"

May tried those too. Search after search, going through everything that felt relevant to the case, or that their research had uncovered so far.

No matter what she chose, she couldn't find more information on the fact she was almost remembering. Nothing except that persistent nagging in her mind, telling her that there really was something to be found, if only she could look properly.

She entered Jessop's name.

That, too, produced no results. May was frustrated. What if she just couldn't remember? What if it was something that wasn't searchable, something that she'd only heard about through chitchat in the community, or her mother telling her?

"Let's try all the victims' family names. Maybe that brings something up."

"Okay." Owen sounded quietly hopeful, which was more than May felt.

They both did the search. May stared as the results flashed in, willing for something to appear. But there was nothing significant. Weddings, funerals, special events. Once, Shawna's dad had served on the mayoral committee and once, Emily's mother had been involved in a road rage incident, but it had been handled long ago and although May searched carefully, the offender seemed to have been a passerby who had left town.

She sighed. She'd had hopes for the road rage incident, but nothing was getting anywhere.

"I'm sorry. I'm sorry," May said. "I just can't think. We've run out of ideas. Maybe we need a break. Maybe we need to stop, get some fresh air, clear our heads."

She knew they couldn't. There was no time for that. They couldn't do so much as take a breath when the clock was ticking inexorably on.

"Let's not search names. Let's search places," he decided.

"The town. Chestnut Hill?" May asked.

"Or maybe even more specific. The school. Chestnut Hill High. That's where all the victims are from. There could be a common thread here we're not seeing," Owen suggested.

"Let's take a look."

They each keyed in the name of the town and the high school.

May's shoulders felt stiff and her eyes were strained from speed-reading irrelevant information on that bright, unforgiving screen. She felt as if this was the last possible lead. She could not think of any other possibilities.

"No, this is it," May said. "This is our last chance."

She stared at the screen, willing it to bring up something that might be helpful.

May's first impression, looking at the collective body of news, was that it was definitely interesting.

"One thing I'm seeing here is that bullying has been a problem at the school for longer than I thought, but it's flared up recently," May said. There were a couple of incidents where parents had gone to the media, and where teachers had spoken out.

However, bullying was not an exclusive problem of Chestnut Hill High alone. Many schools faced similar issues, May knew, and she couldn't see how they could make a connection between that and the crimes.

"Drugs are a problem, too. There are a couple of incidents of drugs. But I guess for any school these days, that's also not unusual. You're never going to be able to control it totally," Owen said.

"These are serious problems, without a doubt. But I'm not finding anything that links them to these crimes in a way we can take forward," she said.

They stared into each other's eyes. Neither of them seemed ready to give up.

May scrolled back another page just to make sure.

And then she landed on an article that at first didn't ring any bells. Then, suddenly, it did. She looked at the name, and the name was familiar. The name brought it all back to her, just like that.

"Here it is, Owen. I've found it," she said excitedly. "This is what I was thinking of, what was nagging at my mind. But it was longer ago than I thought. Years ago. This happened just after I joined the police. That's why I heard about it but I wasn't really involved."

"And what is it?"

May read out the headline. *"Chestnut Hill High Student Commits Suicide. Bullying Cited as the Cause."*

"So a teen committed suicide due to bullying?"

"Penelope Jackson was on a school sports team, and a good academic student. But bullying drove this lacrosse star to take her life," May read.

"Lacrosse?" Owen raised his eyebrows.

"Yes, if I remember correctly, which I'm now starting to do, she was the team captain," May said. Goosebumps prickled her spine. The pieces were starting to fall into place for her now. Was this the critical information they needed to solve this case?

"So she was a well-respected student there, in spite of whatever she was going through that caused her suicide?"

"She was a very talented athlete and good academically, but you know how bullying is. Sometimes that doesn't make a difference. It was the other students who were the problem."

"That's very sad," Owen observed.

"I think we need to look into this. Let's see what we can find on this case. The lacrosse angle is a link, and it's significant to me that all of the victims who have been taken were involved in bullying. Both Shawna and Emily were accused of it. And although Chanel's mother said she was not a bully, she did say that people from that school got sent home during the day for that reason."

Owen nodded. "So someone watching the school might have thought she was."

"Let's find out the details," May decided. "Let's see where the Jacksons are now, and take a closer look at exactly what played out with this incident. It was long ago, but sometimes things brew. Something could have triggered somebody to start killing now."

CHAPTER TWENTY EIGHT

May felt this newly discovered angle was her last chance. It was the only other possibility she could think of. Nothing else seemed viable, or linked the victims together.

With the victims all attending the same school, there was already a common thread. This was not a random selection of young women. Chestnut Hill High was being targeted by the killer, most definitely. And he wasn't just picking them up outside the school gates. Shawna, for instance, had gone out running and disappeared from there. She hadn't been taken while leaving the school. So the killer had known who she was. She had been singled out and followed.

At least, May strongly suspected so, and she was going to go forward with this premise as the most likely.

With this important fact in mind, May set out to read up on the case she dimly remembered from her earlier years as a trainee police officer.

Strangely enough, that moment when she'd heard the news about Penelope had been one of her most vivid memories at the time. It had resonated with her.

She'd recently failed the FBI entrance exam. She'd been hurting and ashamed, feeling inadequate compared to Kerry, who had been the top candidate accepted two years previously.

As a new officer in the local department, May had been learning the ropes, which had often consisted at that time of doing all the tasks nobody else had time for or wanted to do.

May remembered that before she joined, the Fairshore police department had been much messier and more disorganized. Sheriff Jack had spruced it up and done a major clean-out. May's job at the time had been to go through mountains of dusty paperwork, organizing the files into bundles and making sure all the information was correct before being sent to the archives.

Thinking back, she clearly remembered the smell of dust from those early days.

She'd been toiling over the files when she'd heard the call come in.

"Sheriff!" the officer at the front desk had called. "You need to go to Chestnut Hill. There's been a suicide! A seventeen-year-old girl has killed herself!"

Listening to the words, May had felt her heart clench.

At a low point herself, she'd felt so terrible for this young girl, her whole future ahead of her.

She'd stared down at the files, tears prickling her eyes, as she wished, too late, that the girl had shared her predicament and been able to get help.

Vulnerable herself at that time, she felt the case lance into her heart.

And May thought it was for that reason that she deliberately hadn't looked for any further details or read up on it at all. She'd blocked it out, not wanting to feel that sadness again. Chestnut Hill was in a different local jurisdiction; the Fairshore police hadn't been involved beyond the sheriff's callout.

Now, reading on, she learned more about what had played out.

"*Penelope Jackson had been a victim of bullying*," May read from the news report, her voice shaking slightly. "*She left a suicide note behind in which she said she could no longer stand being harassed by girls in her class.*"

"That's terrible," Owen said.

"She took the family's old rowboat to the lake, where she sailed out onto the waters and overdosed on sleeping tablets. By the time she was found, she was already dead. Her family described themselves as 'heartbroken' by the terrible incident."

Owen gasped. "But that's so similar to what happened at these murder scenes."

"It is," May agreed. "Owen, this has to be behind it. It has to. It's just too similar in too many ways. Someone knew about this incident. Someone had it in mind. I'm convinced of it. And I'm wondering if it could be Penelope's father."

She summarized more from the article. "The suicide note stated that Penelope had been mocked because of her family. She'd stepped down as captain of the lacrosse team after other girls had complained, and refused to be on the team."

"How disgusting of them!" Owen said.

"Bullies can be so cruel," May agreed. "And what's also clear is that the school was not doing enough to manage the problem."

"What else does it say?"

"Her few friends spoke out to say she was threatened and her belongings were thrown around the locker room. The bullies stole her school books and even made up a letter, pretending to be from Penelope herself, saying that she was doing all this to herself because of her 'weird' parents."

"Why were the parents weird?" Owen asked.

"It says here the father was a survivalist who was trying to isolate from society out in the woods. Her parents were divorced, and her mother had remarried to a logger who apparently had a criminal record, but the article is not clear on what it was. But apparently all of that was a reason for terrible bullying at school."

"Seriously?" Owen said.

"There's an editor's note here to say that the mother subsequently left her second husband after Penelope's suicide. She moved out of state."

"So that's a hugely tragic story. But it means there are two suspects who could have done this, doesn't it?"

"Yes. Penelope's real father and also her stepfather. Both of them would have gone through trauma and both of them would have had the right resources and materials to be able to reconstruct the scene. Because that is what sounds like might have happened."

"What do we know about them?"

Crowding around the screen again, May looked up both the men.

"Mr. Jackson lives in the woods north of Chestnut Hill. He has a cabin there on the shores of the lake. And the stepfather, Abner Delaforte, lives on a small farm outside of town. I think that area also borders the lake."

May thought to herself that both of these sounded like isolated spots. If either of the men had taken Chanel South, she could be held here at this moment.

If they were not the right suspects then there would be no harm done in looking. The chances were good that if Jessop really was guilty, he would crack under Kerry's intense questioning.

But if there was a chance of saving a life in the meantime, May knew that as a local cop, she had to do her duty for the community.

"We've got to go, I think," she said to Owen.

"That's what I'm thinking, too. We have to see if she's there."

What to do about Kerry? May wondered, as Owen tapped keys on the laptop, bringing up an area map.

Her sister had stated very firmly that there were to be no more interruptions. She was at a critical psychological moment in her questioning. And so far, May and Owen had no proof, only a strong theory.

"I think we shouldn't interrupt Kerry during her interrogation. Not unless we're sure," she decided, and Owen nodded, looking relieved.

"And we're not sure yet. For a start, we have two different suspects. So, let's head out on our own and find out more about them both."

"The problem is that they are in completely opposite directions. These two locations are about thirty miles from each other, and the one in the woods will take a long time to get to, as it will be over very rough tracks."

May saw what he was saying.

Going together to each location would take them a couple of hours. It would waste precious time, which they might not have, because this killer was speeding up his interval.

"We're going to have to split up," she said.

Owen nodded. "Yes. We're going to have to do that to have the best chance of saving her if she's out there."

"Which one do you want to take?" May decided to give him the choice. She couldn't see there was much of a difference. Both were isolated, rural spots. Both of them might end up with May and Owen coming face to face with people who distrusted the law. There was potential danger in both situations.

But May already knew which one Owen was going to choose. She knew without a doubt that he was going to volunteer to go to the stepfather, because he had a criminal record.

Having a record made him more potentially dangerous and a more likely suspect.

"I'll take Abner Delaforte, if you don't mind," Owen said, confirming what May had thought. She felt a twist of worry that he was putting himself in danger. The only positive was that Mr. Jackson's cabin was closer to where they were now, even though it was going to be a rough drive there. If she got there, and it checked out, she could rush to help him, even if it took a while.

"I'll go out to Mr. Jackson and check his place. Let's stay in touch every step of the way and do what we can."

May knew that wouldn't be much. This was a small police department. There was no readily available backup that could be called out to support them on what was no more than a hunch.

It would be only herself and Owen, heading out into possible danger.

But perhaps, if they were lucky, one of them would find the captured victim before she, too, was killed.

CHAPTER TWENTY NINE

May gripped the wheel as she neared the woodlands cabin where she hoped Mr. Jackson might be found. Trees scraped and brushed the sides and roof of the car as she headed in and out of the dappled shade.

She drove as fast as she could, feeling anxious about Owen. She wanted to be able to rule this suspect out in time to help him, if he needed her help.

She felt worried that her partner was heading out to come face to face with a man who had a criminal record, and who had lost his wife as well as his stepchild, due to the disaster of the Chestnut Hill High bullying.

She was not downplaying the likelihood that she might also confront the killer, but she was very aware that Owen would have put himself in the path of the most dangerous scenario.

Make sure you take care, Owen, she thought.

May didn't know what it was like to lose a child, but she knew what it was like to lose a sister. The pain, the memories, never left you. And perhaps it had taken the killer years to recover from the pain and to plan his revenge.

Or perhaps it was just that there had been a few recent incidents of bullying in the news, and it had pushed him over the edge mentally, pushed him past breaking point, into a murderous mindset where he'd gone on a killing spree because in his own damaged mind, he felt it was the only way to stop this.

May gunned the engine, but then braked hard as she reached the point where she had to turn off the worn, potholed blacktop and onto the sandy, rutted track that led to the cabin. She tried to make sure that her mind was calm and clear, not distracted and bogged down in worry. She had to be at her most focused now. She needed to be a sharp cop, one who could make the right decisions.

But right now, May felt vulnerable.

She felt vulnerable not only because she might be facing a man who had killed multiple times, but because she was going into it alone. That meant a lot of responsibility rested on her shoulders. She didn't want to fail. She could not afford to miss a detail that might lead her to the captured girl, and she could not afford to mess up.

May felt terrified that their brave attempt at rescue might somehow end in disaster, and that she would be the deputy who had failed the community. She had to save this girl, to do what she could to put a stop to this evil.

She had to be the best cop that she could be.

Driving along the zigzagging track, heading ever deeper into the woods, May glanced at the map and saw she was nearly there. The cabin was on the other side of this steep ridge, which would then veer sharply downhill toward the hidden shores of a peninsula of the lake.

May slowed to a crawl as she crested the ridge, nursing the car down the rutted, washed out road. She could see the cabin ahead. It was a small, humble building, set in surroundings that were utterly alone.

She scrambled out of the car, feeling intensely nervous as she stared at the small cabin ahead. Was Chanel hidden here? Or was she being held captive at the farmhouse that Owen was speeding toward?

May felt like a mess of emotions as she walked to the humble cabin, with her shoes slipping and sliding along the uneven, stony track. She stepped with care, picking her way while going as fast as she could. She didn't want to lose her footing and tumble down the hillside.

She steeled herself for what she might find, knowing she would have to be ready for whatever came her way.

She had one advantage, of course. She was a police officer and she had a gun. But having a gun came with strict rules and responsibilities. If you shot it, you were accountable. You could not threaten innocent citizens without good cause.

Here was the cabin. Her breath was rasping, ragged in her throat, as she reached it.

It was much prettier than she'd imagined the hideaway of a survivalist to be.

It was nicely finished, with a front porch and a front lawn lined with flowerbeds. May could even see a porch swing on the wooden boards. There were solar panels on the sunny side of the roof.

She could see a small garden with vegetables growing. The grass was neatly mowed, and the flowerbeds were weeded. Someone was proud of this home and had taken care in keeping it well.

And there was that someone, outside. May's heart sped up as she saw him.

The man was kneeling, digging in the garden, and he looked up in surprise when he saw her.

"Hello!" he said, rocking back on his heels as he stared at her. He was a slim man, average height. He was wearing faded jeans and an old T-shirt, and May saw he was holding a small trowel.

Nothing about him rang alarm bells with her, and he looked to be every inch a normal citizen.

"I'm Deputy Moore," she introduced herself.

"I'm Mr. Jackson. Is everything okay? Why are you here?"

He had a friendly smile, despite the anxious note she could hear in his words, May thought. When he smiled, and his face softened, she found herself smiling back. He definitely didn't look like a madman or a killer, or someone who would have kept a grudge for years before exploding in a series of murders. He just looked to be a garden-loving man who had built himself a hideaway.

Or was he? May reminded herself sharply that she could take nothing for granted.

"May I ask a few questions?" she asked, trying to sound calm and matter-of-fact, and not give away how nervous she felt.

"Of course. But what's this about?"

"We've been researching the recent cases where Chestnut Hill High students have been murdered and abducted. We're seeking information. I read a news report that your daughter committed suicide years ago," May said. "I was wondering if there were any links to the current tragedies, or if you could help us with any facts."

She wasn't going to accuse him of the crimes. But she was watching him carefully as she spoke. He was definitely remaining calm, and didn't seem worried by her words.

"I don't go into town much. I'm so sorry to hear about that." His eyes were pale blue. In his slightly lined face, they exuded sympathy. His voice was gentle. "I know it's terrible. I know it's devastating. I will never recover from my own loss. But I don't know of anyone who would do that."

"Would you mind if I came in and asked you a few questions?" May asked, hoping that this would allow her to see the interior of this small cabin.

"Not at all," Mr. Jackson said.

He led the way into the cabin.

It was small, neat, and tidy. May couldn't see anywhere that anyone might be concealed. The main room was a small kitchen–living room. Off it was a bathroom and a bedroom. The doors to both were open. It seemed like a calm place. Until you noticed the handgun on the shelf and the hunting rifle by the door.

But this man was a survivalist. He would have guns, and guns had not been used in the murders.

May felt satisfied that she'd checked it out. There was nothing that seemed untoward here. She'd better ask some questions, though, so that she could justify having invited herself inside.

"Do you still have contact with anyone at the school?" she asked.

He shook his head. "I deliberately broke off contact there."

"Have you been in town the past few days?" she asked.

"I haven't. I don't often go. I don't need to. I'm very self-sufficient here. I prefer not to be around people. Perhaps you can see why. I've always been a loner."

"I guess I do see why," she said.

This man lived alone. She couldn't confirm his claims that he'd been here the past few days, but nor could she prove they were false.

She noticed a laptop set up on the table, though. So he definitely was connected with the outside world. With the internet at his fingertips, he could easily have researched who the students were that he wanted to target, and gone into town and followed them.

A hammer and a saw in a box below the table brought to mind making those wooden rafts. But that again was standard equipment for someone in a log cabin, living off the grid.

On the mantelpiece above the fireplace, there were about fifteen framed photos. All of Penelope. May stared at the faded prints.

Penelope in her lacrosse shoes, captured in full run. She was a short girl, a little over five foot. Small and petite for her age compared to the others.

Penelope in a blue shirt, smiling at the camera in a school sports team photograph.

With a squeeze of her heart, May realized exactly how much this daughter had meant to her father.

She needed to look past his softly spoken front, and she needed to recognize the man beneath. This man could be the killer. He could have Chanel hidden somewhere right now. But the photos alone were not enough reason to pull her gun and start threatening him. He could simply deny everything.

Chanel was not in this cabin. Where did he have her, and how could she find out?

She didn't have enough evidence to go on. Just a very strong feeling she needed to discover more. Direct questioning would get her nowhere. If she arrested this man and took him in, he might not talk.

And that meant they might never find Chanel, because who knew where in these vast woods she was hidden?

May decided she needed to resort to the investigator's version of sleight of hand.

She needed to allow him to make the next move. She needed to pretend everything was normal, and that this man was not a suspect. She had to turn and leave. Pretend to go. And then she had to see what happened, and if Mr. Jackson headed out to find and kill his third victim.

CHAPTER THIRTY

"Thank you so much for your time," May said. Her stomach was churning as she turned and walked out of the cabin, hoping that her bluff would work, and that her hunch was correct. She headed up the hill, back to her car. She was feeling tense inside as she climbed in and started it up. She turned around and drove it along the steep track. But she only went far enough to be out of earshot. Then she looked for a place to hide the car.

May hoped she was far enough away that he couldn't hear the sound of the engine amid these muffling trees. She veered off the track and drove as far into the trees as she could. She killed the engine and climbed out.

And then she climbed back down the track, returning to the house.

May walked as quietly as she could, feeling breathless with anxiety, still racked with doubt over whether coming back for a final check was the right thing to do, or just a dangerous waste of time.

But she had to see what was happening. She had to see if there was a chance she could find and save Chanel.

She knew there was a chance she could be wrong. He could well be a perfectly innocent man. This could all be a wild goose chase. But her gut instincts were screaming for her to return, and it might just be because she was onto something.

There was the house, looking as peaceful as it had before. The front door was partway open. May crept toward it. Was he in there?

The house was empty. She looked more closely. Everything was the way it had been. The doors were open, and she could see into the bedroom and into the tiny bathroom.

But he was gone.

He'd gone to find her, she was sure of it.

She'd taken too long. She'd lost him. He was already on his way to her. Without wasting a moment, he'd headed out into the woods to go and get her.

May felt her heart accelerate. How could she find him? He could have gone in any direction. It was too late. Her chance had gone.

Unless—unless there was one last-ditch attempt she could make.

It wasn't a great idea; in fact, May knew it wasn't even a good idea. But it was her only idea. What she was about to do would be dangerous, for sure. But it might lead her to Chanel, and if it didn't, it might lead him back to her again.

She walked out of the house.

She drew in a breath, as long and deep as she could.

If she was wrong, she was going to be in trouble which she hoped she'd be able to handle.

But if she was right, then it might make all the difference.

"Chanel!" she screamed, at the top of her voice. "Chanel! Are you here? Can you hear me? Chanel? I'm coming to help you!"

The woods resounded with silence. But then, finally, she had her answer.

From somewhere deep in the trees, May heard a faint, faraway cry in reply.

She'd been answered! And the voice was coming from the left!

She raced along the narrow track. This was where he had her. Somewhere deep in these woods. Breath burned in her throat as she ran. He could be preparing to kill her now. She had to get there in time.

"Chanel!" she screamed again. She took out her gun, knowing she might have to burst into this hiding place to make the rescue.

The trees lining the track grew thicker the further away they got from the lake. They twisted together to form a dark canopy. Roots and vines snaked along the ground. It was like a tunnel, and May raced along it.

And then, behind her, she heard a massive roar, the screaming of an engine.

The next moment, from around a bend in the path, an ATV accelerated toward her. She glimpsed him at the wheel, his face intent as he sped along the path.

He'd heard her all right, and he was going to destroy the threat she represented. He was going to run her down!

There was no time for a clear shot. The ATV's engine screamed in her ears. May dove for cover. She literally threw herself to the side, tumbling into the trees, branches scratching and scraping her.

Bumping and rocking, the ATV screamed past. It caught a tree branch which slammed into her, knocking her off her feet and sending her tumbling down the mossy slope. But she was still alive. He'd missed her by a hair's breadth. And he was plowing forward, not turning back to try again.

That was the good news. The bad news was that she'd lost her gun in the fall. It was somewhere in the mass of bushes and ferns. She had no idea where it might have landed, and didn't have time to hunt for it. Not when he was clearly on the way to his victim.

And that was the worst news. Because if he wasn't coming back for her, it meant he was heading out to do the final kill, continuing with his deadly mission right now.

May scrambled to her feet, her hands bleeding from the cuts and scratches. She sprinted along the path.

There, ahead of her, near a sheltered part of the lake, was a tiny cabin. It was invisible in the trees. This was where he must be holding her.

And outside the cabin was a rustic, homemade raft. It stood near the shores of the lake. She felt ice-cold as she saw it.

He had prepared the scene for his final victim. But because she'd interfered, because he was in a hurry, he was doing things differently this time.

May caught her breath as she saw him carrying the struggling girl out. He had her in his arms. She was fighting against him. But he was a strong man, despite his slim build, and he was carrying her with ease.

He didn't notice May. Perhaps he thought she'd been injured worse than she had been. She'd always been a good faller and knew how to roll. He was intent on getting his victim back to the lakeside, to the raft. To the end of her days. She could see Chanel fighting. She was screaming. Fear distorted her face. She had probably seen his killing cabin, the raft, and she was desperately afraid.

May raced down the hill. She left the path and ran out on to the grass in the clearing by the cabin.

Ahead, she saw him place the girl onto the raft. He was wrestling with ropes to tie her.

"Drop her!" May screamed. "Leave her be!"

He turned in her direction, and his face was different now. Furious and intent.

But the moment's distraction had been enough. Chanel pulled away from him, crying in fear.

"Go!" May shouted. "Run!"

Looking around in panic, May realized there was nowhere for her to run. Nowhere that he could not easily outrun her.

With a terrified shriek, Chanel turned and plunged into the lake, swimming away from him.

She swam like an Olympic athlete, fear giving her strength. He threw down the ropes and ran after her, his feet slipping in the mud as he raced along the lakeside. Then he leaped into the water, heading out toward her.

"No!" May screeched. She didn't hesitate. Reaching the lake, she launched herself into the water and swam with all her might toward him.

He was a better runner than swimmer. Or perhaps it was the heavy boots he was wearing. She managed to catch his foot, clinging onto that solid boot. She held on with all her might, but he kicked out viciously.

She was flung away, tumbling through the water, coughing. The impact slammed her against the side of the raft.

And then, with an angry snarl, he turned back toward her. He grabbed her, his hands tightening in her hair.

May only had a moment to draw in a breath before the killer attacked her, pushing her down, forcing her head under the clear, cold waters of the lake.

His hands felt like steel. May struggled for all she was worth. He was going to drown her. She had been right to suspect him. And now she would die.

He was going to kill her unless, somehow, she could stop him. But she was running out of air, and she knew if she wasn't able to fight him off in the next few moments, she would have to take in a breath, and would drown.

CHAPTER THIRTY ONE

Always do the unexpected.

Those words of good advice suddenly came back to May's panicked and oxygen-starved brain. Kerry had been the master at that. If you fought with Kerry, best you had backup plans B, C, and D for when she managed to shock you with something that should not actually have been possible.

It was time for May to take that good advice, and save her life, because otherwise, that iron hand would keep her underwater. Both she and Chanel would die.

Instead of struggling away, she flung herself toward the man, grabbing for his legs. His arms squeezed her tighter, and their bodies rolled together in the water. Hoping to surprise and knock him off-balance, she locked her hands around his thigh, digging her fingers in as hard as she could. She punched him in the back of the knee with her other hand, hoping to find a pressure point, praying for a miracle.

He flinched, staggered, and his grip loosened. She pulled away. And suddenly, she was back up to the surface.

May gasped in a breath. Then she started choking and coughing. But she was alive.

She kicked out at him viciously, wanting to reinforce the small advantage she'd obtained.

However, he wasn't fighting her. Not anymore. Instead, he was rushing to shore, and as she watched, he sprinted up the path toward the cabin.

It was not a far way to go, and she knew what he was seeking. He was going to get the shotgun that she'd seen propped against the wall by the door. He was going to destroy her, fast and efficiently. She wouldn't be able to get to him before he got to his shotgun, and her own gun was lying somewhere in the woods. She had nothing to fight him with. And she needed to get Chanel to a safer place somehow. That was a priority, before he came back with the gun.

Where was Chanel?

Looking around frantically, May saw she'd swum back to shore, a good distance away.

"Wait!" May screeched. Her voice was barely audible. Drenched vocal cords. She tried again.

"Chanel!" she yelled.

This time, she heard.

Chanel turned, her eyes wide with fear and desperation, her hair dripping onto her face, her shirt clinging to her body, her jeans water-stained.

May scrambled from the water. Her clothes were soaking wet. She ran to Chanel, feeling as if her legs were wobbly and didn't belong to her at all. "Come with me. We need to hide somewhere safe."

"Where?" Chanel asked, her voice panicked.

"I guess in the trees. But we need to hurry! If he sees us, he'll start shooting."

May had no idea where they should go. She just knew that in a few more moments, Jackson was going to erupt from the cabin, armed and dangerous. If they were in the way of that shotgun, it would be bad news.

"This way!" May decided. There was no time for anything clever except to run to the closest cover, because she could already see him coming out.

She grabbed Chanel's arm.

And then she ran, as fast as she could. At first, she had to tug Chanel along, but then, as the girl recovered and found her strength, she powered alongside May.

They burst into the tree line. Looking around for the best cover, May saw a deadfall, propped up against a solid-looking boulder.

"Here!" May pushed Chanel behind the rock.

"What are we doing?" Chanel sounded breathless.

"Hiding quietly," May hissed.

A cracking sound split the air and Chanel squawked as a tree branch a few yards to the right fell down with a crashing sound.

"Try not to make a noise," May whispered, her heart hammering.

"I'll try," Chanel whispered back in a shaking voice. "But this is scary. Is he coming our way? What's he doing now?"

"I'm not sure," May admitted.

Then she heard him calling, in a weird, wheedling tone.

"It's all okay," he said. "You'll be safe. Trust me. I won't hurt you. I have no intention of doing that. You'll be okay."

"He's mad," Chanel whispered. "That's what he said to me also. Then he stared going on about how I was a bully, and it was because of people like me that his daughter had died, and he didn't want to hurt me at all, but he wanted others to learn a lesson." Her voice broke off into a sob.

May was getting a good picture of the killer's intentions. This was sadly how he had been scarred from the terrible experience of losing his daughter. Gradually, the hurt had festered until it erupted in a murderous spree where he targeted other suspected bullies and killed them.

It was a pity that this information was coming at a time when they were likely to be gunned down at any moment.

"Do you have a gun?" Chanel whispered.

"Um, no," May admitted. "I lost hold of it when he tried to run me down with his ATV."

But that question gave her an idea.

He would most definitely want to shoot May. But perhaps, if she was able to distract him, this deranged man might not shoot Chanel just yet. Not if she could get into his mind and press the right buttons. And she thought she knew what they were, and how she might be able to buy some time.

"I think we need to try something," she whispered.

"What's that?"

"It might not work. But this man is going to shoot us otherwise."

They flinched, as a tree the other side of them took a hit, bark exploding everywhere. The sound was deafening. May's ears were ringing from the blast.

"What can we do?" Chanel hissed, sounding panicked.

"You need to stay calm and call out to him. Say that I'm trying to hurt you. Say that he must come and save you."

Chanel's eyes widened. "That? You think he'll listen?"

"I have no idea," May admitted. "He might not. But things can't get worse for us. He's already guessed where we are."

She flinched as a closer tree blasted under the impact. She could hear his footsteps now, crunching closer.

"You don't need to worry," he called.

"I—I'll try. I guess I have to," Chanel whispered. "But what will you do?"

"I'll try to get around behind him. You go over this side of the deadfall. Make him look there. I'll go the far side."

Chanel swallowed. Then she nodded.

May crept over to the edge of the deadfall. And then, in a trembling voice, Chanel called, "Help me! The policewoman is hurting me!"

There was absolute silence from beyond.

"She's hurting me. Come and get me!" Chanel called.

May could see this had struck a chord in the delusional man's mind. For a moment at least, he was distracted from the killing mindset that was forcing him to slaughter his terrified victims.

With his attention hopefully focused the other way, May dropped to the ground and wriggled out from the deadfall, keeping as low as possible as she wormed her way through the undergrowth, feeling intensely vulnerable now that there was no protection between him and her. Any shotgun blast would drill straight through her in an instant.

But Chanel was doing a fantastic job. Her voice was as false and plaintive as his had been. May could hear she was imitating someone. Perhaps she was remembering the pleas of her younger sister whom she'd tried so hard to protect.

"Oh, please help me! Please come and help me. She's being so cruel! I'm scared!"

And clearly, Jackson was captivated. At any rate, the shotgun had not blasted out again. Perhaps, in the last sane corner of his mind, he was recognizing that there was someone out here he needed to protect.

Hoping she was out of range of his vision, May set off to the nearest tree at a silent run, keeping crouched.

She had made it. Her heart was going at what felt like two hundred beats a minute, but she'd gotten to cover and she was now nearing him. Seemingly hypnotized by Chanel, he was pacing slowly toward her.

May did another run. Reached another tree. Just one more and she would be directly behind him.

She ran. She got to the tree. She was behind him.

He was still moving toward Chanel, who was keeping up her act brilliantly.

"Don't hurt me!" she was pleading. "Please, save me from this woman!"

Now, May had to close in on him while the power of this delusion was keeping him from killing.

She ran closer. Close enough to see the shotgun, still gripped in his hand.

"Where are you?" he asked. "Come out, or I'll shoot. Come out now! Show yourself to me!"

Chanel's charm was wearing off. He was starting to veer back to his original purpose and forgetting the distraction.

It was now or never. May burst out from the screen of greenery. He heard her and started to turn.

The shotgun barrel swung around to her. She saw his face tauten in anger.

And then she reached him, launching at him in a flying tackle. She knocked him to the ground. The shotgun blast went high. In fact, the blast was so loud it was deafening, the gunpowder blast burning her face and stinging her eyes.

She clung to the man with all her strength. They hit the ground together. But May was on top and using her weight and strength against him. She grabbed at the shotgun with both hands, trying to wrest it from his grip. He fought back with all the strength of madness.

For a terrible moment, she thought she wasn't going to be able to do it. She was going to get shot. But finally, she was able to grab the barrel and stab it down toward him. The butt of the gun caught his chin and he flinched.

May grabbed the gun out of his hand. She kneed him in the stomach, choking the breath out of him. He curled up, gasping, coughing.

She had him now. Wrestling the handcuffs off her belt, she got one of his wrists in and then the other. They clicked closed.

May kept a tight grip on them, but she could see the fight had gone out of him. He was dazed, winded, and in pain.

Backup was needed now. She grabbed the phone out of her pocket and made a call.

Owen answered in one ring.

"I'm on my way to you," he gabbled out, sounding stressed. "Where are you? Are you okay?"

"I have him," May said. "I have him. It's over. Call the others. I'll send you the coordinates."

She sent them quickly. Then she closed her eyes, feeling thankful beyond belief that this terrifying takedown had succeeded.

Finally, they had the killer.

And she had done what she thought would be impossible, and had saved his final victim.

CHAPTER THIRTY TWO

An hour later, the entire lakeside area was abuzz with police. May felt astounded that even an FBI helicopter had flown in. Police were swarming the scene and recording evidence. From the stash of sleeping tablets in the cabin, to the stack of wooden logs in the nearby forest, with nails scattered around, and the raft itself by the water's edge, there was no shortage of proof that finally, the killer's lair had been located.

Jackson himself was in an ambulance, sedated and handcuffed, being taken to the hospital for examination before he would be assigned to his longer-term incarceration, ready for court.

Chanel had been quickly debriefed and then examined by the paramedics on the scene. After she was declared to be healthy and unhurt, she'd been collected by her jubilant and tearful parents.

May was so relieved that she had carried her part of the plan out perfectly. At the end, she knew, they had walked a tightrope of risk that had been precarious, and could so easily have gone wrong.

Swathed in Owen's jacket, she had finally stopped shivering from her ordeal in the lake's deep, chilly waters.

"Are you sure you're okay?" he said for the third time.

"I'm fine," May said.

They were seated under a tree. May had wanted to help, but she was under strict instructions from the paramedic team to get warm and dry first. She already felt warm, and she would soon be dry. She was well hydrated thanks to the bottles of water Owen had brought her, and she knew that in another minute, she would be ready to head into the scene and complete her reports.

And she had to admit, there was no shortage of help in the meantime.

"Are you sure you're okay?"

May looked up. This time, the question came from Sheriff Jack.

"I'm fine," she said.

"It sounds like you and the captive girl acted in a most heroic and resourceful way to save yourselves," Jack said. "I'm extremely impressed. What you did was a classic example of thinking on your feet and adapting to circumstances. It was so well thought through that I can see this being an example in police textbooks one day."

May felt a thrill of pleasure to hear that.

Kerry, who had been coordinating the search at the cabin, marched over.

"Mom's on the phone," she said. "I told her everything that happened. She wants to know if you're all right."

"I'm fine. But I'll speak to her," May said.

Kerry handed her the phone.

As May stood up to take the call, she surveyed the complex scene, feeling a satisfied thrill. Everyone here was a hero, playing their part.

"May!" Her mother's voice resounded with admiration. "Your sister told me what you did out there in the forest, to make sure that dear Chanel, who we've actually met, was freed. That was amazing. It sounds like something out of the movies. Congratulations, my angel."

To May, the words of praise felt like a warm balm.

"Just doing my job," she said modestly.

"Well, I can't wait to hear all about it and to give you a big hug. Do you think you'll be able to get here for dinner?"

"Sure. It's only five p.m. now. We should be done here in another hour."

"I'll get the roast in the oven, then, and slow cook it. And May?"

"Yes, Mom?"

"Your father sends his love."

May smiled, feeling bemused. Kerry was looking ever so slightly miffed as May handed the phone back.

"It's a team effort, right?" her sister asked.

"Absolutely," May confirmed. "A team effort."

Kerry thought for a moment.

Then she leaned closer.

"By the way," she said, "I haven't forgotten about that key you found in Lauren's evidence box. I know we need to research it, but it seems to be quite difficult. The software isn't translating the label properly and the techs need to make tweaks to it, and the shaft itself could be any of a hundred different possibilities and I won't settle for naming just ten of them. I want to know which." Her chin jutted stubbornly.

"Thank you," May said.

"So, bottom line, I'm working on it. And I'll let you know. I'd better go and wrap up now if we're going to be in time for that roast."

Already focused on the cabin again, Kerry hurried away.

May took a last gulp of water. Then she turned to look at the scene around her.

Everything was under control. Even in her exhaustion, she couldn't help but feel a little smile creasing her face.

The stress of this case was finally over. She had the killer. And he was going to be behind bars for the rest of his life, most likely in a psychiatric prison ward.

May felt a sense of relief. And also of hope. They had solved one crime that was based on an incident from the past, and she felt hopeful that between her and Kerry, they could find out what the key was for.

And then it might take them on the next step of this slow and emotionally painful journey to solve another mystery that lay hidden in the past.

But that was something to think about tomorrow. For now, work called.

"Come on," she said to Owen with a grin, stepping forward. Her shoes were still squelchy, but that was a minor detail, and the late afternoon, though starting to darken, was not cold. "Let's finish up here. We've got a case to wrap up."

EPILOGUE

It was late at night when May finally arrived home. What a day it had been. A capture, a takedown, a rescue. And finally, the event she'd dreaded most of all—a family dinner. Only this time, May had to admit, it hadn't been as excruciating as the ones in the past.

Her parents had been proud of both of them. They'd asked May questions, and that made her feel incredibly happy. They cared. They valued her. She wasn't just the embarrassing afterthought to Kerry's glory.

Immersed in the memories, May only realized after she opened the front door that it hadn't been locked.

She paused, feeling a sudden chill.

May always locked her door. She never forgot to do that. And she clearly remembered locking it before she'd headed out this morning.

What was going on? Had there been a burglary?

It didn't look like the house had been burgled. May went straight to the corner of the living room she used as a study, feeling suddenly breathless with apprehension.

Her laptop was still there. It hadn't been stolen. But it was open on the table. She'd left it packed away.

Hesitantly, May approached. She pressed a key and the screen lit up.

She frowned incredulously. There was a video icon in the middle of the screen that hadn't been there before. Goosebumps prickled her spine as she stared down at it. What was this? What was going on?

Feeling sick with nerves, she pressed Play.

And gasped.

She found herself watching an old, grainy recording. There was her parents' house. It had been taken from the street outside.

May bit her lip.

There were voices coming from inside the house. An argument. She recognized her own voice, raised in anger.

"No!" May sank down onto the chair. Her legs couldn't hold her another moment. This was awful.

It was a recording of the last argument she'd had with Lauren. That terrible fight, after which her eighteen-year-old sister had stormed out of the house, never to be seen again.

There Lauren was. Heading out the front door, looking angry and upset. She clearly hadn't seen whoever was filming. They had been hidden away.

And there was May, marching out after her, yelling a few more insults that she'd forgotten to add when they were inside.

Someone had been watching. Filming. While this happened.

May felt horror fill her at this realization.

And then the screen went blank and a message popped up.

"I'm watching you. I always have been, and I still am. I know what you're trying to do. Back off now. Stop asking questions. This is your last warning. Don't make me act on it."

May buried her head in her hands. Her heart was hammering and she now felt sick with dread.

Kerry had been right when she'd told May that if she went looking for answers, she might run up against people who wanted this secret kept.

Someone had found out she was looking back into Lauren's disappearance. Someone knew more than they should. And that someone was now trying to stop her, using anonymous threats that filled her with dread.

Kerry had warned her that this might happen, and May knew too well that in this small and idyllic community, evil could lurk undiscovered for many years.

May couldn't bear to watch that video again. Couldn't bear to think of this person coming into her private space, setting it up, taunting her with this terrible knowledge, trying to scare her into giving up on the quest for the truth.

She slammed the laptop shut, feeling as if she were living in a nightmare.

But through the trauma and confusion she was feeling, she realized that she had dug down to an unexpected core of steel.

She was not going to let this go. This diabolical threat would not prevent her from learning what had happened. She was going to chase this person down with everything she had.

May raised her tear-stained face.

"You just showed me you exist," she whispered. "And now, I will find you!"

NEVER FORGIVE
(A May Moore Suspense Thriller—Book 5)

From #1 bestselling mystery and suspense author Blake Pierce comes a gripping new series: May Moore, 29, an average Midwestern woman and deputy sheriff, has always lived in the shadow of her older, brilliant FBI agent sister. Yet the sisters are united by the cold case of their missing younger sister—and when a new serial killer strikes in May's quiet, Minnesota lakeside town, it is May's turn to prove herself, to try to outshine her sister and the FBI, and, in this action-packed thriller, to outwit and hunt down a diabolical killer before he strikes again.

"A masterpiece of thriller and mystery."
—Books and Movie Reviews, Roberto Mattos (re Once Gone)

When bodies turn up, the work of a new serial killer, the case seems too easily solved.

But when federal agents storm the killer's lair—only to have it go up in flames and take them with it—May soon realizes that the line is being quickly blurred between the hunter—and the hunted.

A page-turning and harrowing crime thriller featuring a brilliant and tortured Deputy Sheriff, the MAY MOORE series is a riveting mystery, packed with non-stop action, suspense, jaw-dropping twists, and driven by a breakneck pace that will keep you flipping pages late into the night.

Book #6 in the series—NEVER AGAIN—is also available!

"An edge of your seat thriller in a new series that keeps you turning pages! ...So many twists, turns and red herrings... I can't wait to see what happens next."
—Reader review (Her Last Wish)

Blake Pierce

Blake Pierce is the USA Today bestselling author of the RILEY PAGE mystery series, which includes seventeen books. Blake Pierce is also the author of the MACKENZIE WHITE mystery series, comprising fourteen books; of the AVERY BLACK mystery series, comprising six books; of the KERI LOCKE mystery series, comprising five books; of the MAKING OF RILEY PAIGE mystery series, comprising six books; of the KATE WISE mystery series, comprising seven books; of the CHLOE FINE psychological suspense mystery, comprising six books; of the JESSE HUNT psychological suspense thriller series, comprising twenty four books; of the AU PAIR psychological suspense thriller series, comprising three books; of the ZOE PRIME mystery series, comprising six books; of the ADELE SHARP mystery series, comprising sixteen books, of the EUROPEAN VOYAGE cozy mystery series, comprising four books; of the new LAURA FROST FBI suspense thriller, comprising nine books (and counting); of the new ELLA DARK FBI suspense thriller, comprising eleven books (and counting); of the A YEAR IN EUROPE cozy mystery series, comprising nine books, of the AVA GOLD mystery series, comprising six books (and counting); of the RACHEL GIFT mystery series, comprising eight books (and counting); of the VALERIE LAW mystery series, comprising nine books (and counting); of the PAIGE KING mystery series, comprising six books (and counting); of the MAY MOORE mystery series, comprising six books (and counting); and the CORA SHIELDS mystery series, comprising three books (and counting).

An avid reader and lifelong fan of the mystery and thriller genres, Blake loves to hear from you, so please feel free to visit www.blakepierceauthor.com to learn more and stay in touch.

HER LAST HOPE (Book #3)
HER LAST FEAR (Book #4)
HER LAST CHOICE (Book #5)
HER LAST BREATH (Book #6)
HER LAST MISTAKE (Book #7)
HER LAST DESIRE (Book #8)

AVA GOLD MYSTERY SERIES
CITY OF PREY (Book #1)
CITY OF FEAR (Book #2)
CITY OF BONES (Book #3)
CITY OF GHOSTS (Book #4)
CITY OF DEATH (Book #5)
CITY OF VICE (Book #6)

A YEAR IN EUROPE
A MURDER IN PARIS (Book #1)
DEATH IN FLORENCE (Book #2)
VENGEANCE IN VIENNA (Book #3)
A FATALITY IN SPAIN (Book #4)

ELLA DARK FBI SUSPENSE THRILLER
GIRL, ALONE (Book #1)
GIRL, TAKEN (Book #2)
GIRL, HUNTED (Book #3)
GIRL, SILENCED (Book #4)
GIRL, VANISHED (Book 5)
GIRL ERASED (Book #6)
GIRL, FORSAKEN (Book #7)
GIRL, TRAPPED (Book #8)
GIRL, EXPENDABLE (Book #9)
GIRL, ESCAPED (Book #10)
GIRL, HIS (Book #11)

LAURA FROST FBI SUSPENSE THRILLER
ALREADY GONE (Book #1)
ALREADY SEEN (Book #2)
ALREADY TRAPPED (Book #3)
ALREADY MISSING (Book #4)
ALREADY DEAD (Book #5)

ALREADY TAKEN (Book #6)
ALREADY CHOSEN (Book #7)
ALREADY LOST (Book #8)
ALREADY HIS (Book #9)

EUROPEAN VOYAGE COZY MYSTERY SERIES
MURDER (AND BAKLAVA) (Book #1)
DEATH (AND APPLE STRUDEL) (Book #2)
CRIME (AND LAGER) (Book #3)
MISFORTUNE (AND GOUDA) (Book #4)
CALAMITY (AND A DANISH) (Book #5)
MAYHEM (AND HERRING) (Book #6)

ADELE SHARP MYSTERY SERIES
LEFT TO DIE (Book #1)
LEFT TO RUN (Book #2)
LEFT TO HIDE (Book #3)
LEFT TO KILL (Book #4)
LEFT TO MURDER (Book #5)
LEFT TO ENVY (Book #6)
LEFT TO LAPSE (Book #7)
LEFT TO VANISH (Book #8)
LEFT TO HUNT (Book #9)
LEFT TO FEAR (Book #10)
LEFT TO PREY (Book #11)
LEFT TO LURE (Book #12)
LEFT TO CRAVE (Book #13)
LEFT TO LOATHE (Book #14)
LEFT TO HARM (Book #15)
LEFT TO RUIN (Book #16)

THE AU PAIR SERIES
ALMOST GONE (Book#1)
ALMOST LOST (Book #2)
ALMOST DEAD (Book #3)

ZOE PRIME MYSTERY SERIES
FACE OF DEATH (Book#1)
FACE OF MURDER (Book #2)
FACE OF FEAR (Book #3)

FACE OF MADNESS (Book #4)
FACE OF FURY (Book #5)
FACE OF DARKNESS (Book #6)

A JESSIE HUNT PSYCHOLOGICAL SUSPENSE SERIES
THE PERFECT WIFE (Book #1)
THE PERFECT BLOCK (Book #2)
THE PERFECT HOUSE (Book #3)
THE PERFECT SMILE (Book #4)
THE PERFECT LIE (Book #5)
THE PERFECT LOOK (Book #6)
THE PERFECT AFFAIR (Book #7)
THE PERFECT ALIBI (Book #8)
THE PERFECT NEIGHBOR (Book #9)
THE PERFECT DISGUISE (Book #10)
THE PERFECT SECRET (Book #11)
THE PERFECT FAÇADE (Book #12)
THE PERFECT IMPRESSION (Book #13)
THE PERFECT DECEIT (Book #14)
THE PERFECT MISTRESS (Book #15)
THE PERFECT IMAGE (Book #16)
THE PERFECT VEIL (Book #17)
THE PERFECT INDISCRETION (Book #18)
THE PERFECT RUMOR (Book #19)
THE PERFECT COUPLE (Book #20)
THE PERFECT MURDER (Book #21)
THE PERFECT HUSBAND (Book #22)
THE PERFECT SCANDAL (Book #23)
THE PERFECT MASK (Book #24)

CHLOE FINE PSYCHOLOGICAL SUSPENSE SERIES
NEXT DOOR (Book #1)
A NEIGHBOR'S LIE (Book #2)
CUL DE SAC (Book #3)
SILENT NEIGHBOR (Book #4)
HOMECOMING (Book #5)
TINTED WINDOWS (Book #6)

KATE WISE MYSTERY SERIES

IF SHE KNEW (Book #1)
IF SHE SAW (Book #2)
IF SHE RAN (Book #3)
IF SHE HID (Book #4)
IF SHE FLED (Book #5)
IF SHE FEARED (Book #6)
IF SHE HEARD (Book #7)

THE MAKING OF RILEY PAIGE SERIES
WATCHING (Book #1)
WAITING (Book #2)
LURING (Book #3)
TAKING (Book #4)
STALKING (Book #5)
KILLING (Book #6)

RILEY PAIGE MYSTERY SERIES
ONCE GONE (Book #1)
ONCE TAKEN (Book #2)
ONCE CRAVED (Book #3)
ONCE LURED (Book #4)
ONCE HUNTED (Book #5)
ONCE PINED (Book #6)
ONCE FORSAKEN (Book #7)
ONCE COLD (Book #8)
ONCE STALKED (Book #9)
ONCE LOST (Book #10)
ONCE BURIED (Book #11)
ONCE BOUND (Book #12)
ONCE TRAPPED (Book #13)
ONCE DORMANT (Book #14)
ONCE SHUNNED (Book #15)
ONCE MISSED (Book #16)
ONCE CHOSEN (Book #17)

MACKENZIE WHITE MYSTERY SERIES
BEFORE HE KILLS (Book #1)
BEFORE HE SEES (Book #2)
BEFORE HE COVETS (Book #3)
BEFORE HE TAKES (Book #4)

BEFORE HE NEEDS (Book #5)
BEFORE HE FEELS (Book #6)
BEFORE HE SINS (Book #7)
BEFORE HE HUNTS (Book #8)
BEFORE HE PREYS (Book #9)
BEFORE HE LONGS (Book #10)
BEFORE HE LAPSES (Book #11)
BEFORE HE ENVIES (Book #12)
BEFORE HE STALKS (Book #13)
BEFORE HE HARMS (Book #14)

AVERY BLACK MYSTERY SERIES
CAUSE TO KILL (Book #1)
CAUSE TO RUN (Book #2)
CAUSE TO HIDE (Book #3)
CAUSE TO FEAR (Book #4)
CAUSE TO SAVE (Book #5)
CAUSE TO DREAD (Book #6)

KERI LOCKE MYSTERY SERIES
A TRACE OF DEATH (Book #1)
A TRACE OF MURDER (Book #2)
A TRACE OF VICE (Book #3)
A TRACE OF CRIME (Book #4)
A TRACE OF HOPE (Book #5)

Printed in the USA
CPSIA information can be obtained
at www.ICGtesting.com
LVHW040604060624
782431LV00003B/233